All is

Merri and Bright

Tifani Clark

All is Merri and Bright by Tifani Clark
© Tifani Clark 2015

Cover Design: Tifani Clark
Cover image © via iStock.com/arekmalang
Photo ID: 2909889

ISBN-13: 978-0692530856
ISBN-10: 0692530851

An ABCD Publishing Book

http://www.tifaniclark.blogspot.com

Dedicated to my parents and siblings and the memorable Christmases we spent together.

Other books in the Holiday Novella Collection

One Night at Dornea Pines (Halloween 2015)
A Little Bit of Luck (St. Patrick's Day 2016)
Losing Independence (4th of July 2016)

Other books by Tifani Clark

Shadow of a Life
Haven Waiting
On Liberty's Watch

TABLE OF CONTENTS

All is
Merri and Bright

Tifani Clark

Chapter 1

Merri Wilcox could trace her dislike for Brighton Stansbury all the way back to the first grade. Their teacher had introduced him to the class as a new student and then promptly assigned him to sit in the seat next to her. She'd leaned over in her seat and whispered so only he could hear, "Are you named after that skiing place? I've never heard of a person named that." She sincerely wondered, but her first grade self lacked tact.

Brighton responded by sticking his tongue out and tugging on her ponytail. The nerve! *No one* touched Merri's hair without her permission. Some would argue that Merri was technically to blame for starting the years of hatred and disgust, but who wants to get technical? Definitely not Merri. The mutual dislike and teasing that commenced with that one incident followed them all the way through elementary school, continued in junior high, and on into high school. He'd pull a prank on her, and she'd turn around and pull a prank on him. Back and forth, around and around.

She hadn't seen him since he left Salt Lake City to attend one of the Ivy League universities back east somewhere. She couldn't remember which one and to be honest, she didn't care. She'd been Brighton free for seven blissful years.

And that's why Merri gasped when she saw who walked through the door of her hair salon four days before Christmas. Her hands clenched into fists and she barely stopped herself from chopping off a lock of Mrs. Baker's hair in her surprise—or maybe it was dismay. Lacking any better ideas, she instantly dropped to the floor.

"Merri, are you okay?" Paige, another stylist, called from across the room.

"I'm fine. I just dropped a contact." Merri cringed as she knelt in the wispy gray hairs scattered across the floor. *Bad day to wear black pants.*

"But you don't wear—" Paige started to say.

"Shh!" Merri hissed, still crouched behind Mrs. Baker's chair. "I'm not here."

Paige shook her head and set her comb down before stepping to the counter. "Can I help you?" Merri heard her ask.

"I hope so. I've been told the owner of this place is the best in town. Is that you?"

Merri knew that voice all too well. Although it had deepened and matured slightly, the sound would never leave her.

Paige laughed and flipped her hair over her shoulder in a flirtatious way. "I'm not the owner, but you're right—she's great."

"Does she have any appointments available for today?" Brighton asked. "I just need a quick trim."

From her perch under Mrs. Baker's chair, Merri saw Paige hesitate and look over her shoulder. "Uhh...the owner had to step—"

Brighton stepped to the side and looked around Paige. "Merri Wilcox? Is that really you?" he interrupted.

Merri slowly straightened, keeping her back toward the counter as she attempted to brush the gray hair clippings from her pants. "Brighton," she said cordially. Her salon, *The Cut*, had only been open for three months. She didn't want to ruin the success she'd had so far by killing a customer so she carefully set her scissors down before approaching the counter. "Can I help you?"

"Maybe. I was hoping to talk to the owner, but I guess she's not here right now. Maybe you could—"

"Actually, I'm the owner," she cut him off. "You can speak to me." *Why does he bring out the worst in me? I'm usually nice. I like everyone—except him.*

"Really? This is your place? That's great." Brighton grinned. "Looks like life's been good to you since high school."

Merri took in his expensive-looking suit and the fancy sports car parked at the curb outside. She wanted to say something about life *always* being good to him, but she bit her tongue. The less she said, the quicker she could get him out of her salon.

When she didn't say anything else, Brighton continued. "I haven't been back in the area for very long, but I've heard your salon does a great job. Do you have time to give me a quick trim?"

3

Merri's eyes flitted to Brighton's hair. The idea of running her hands through his dark hair made her stomach twist itself into knots. She wanted to say no, but couldn't come up with a good enough excuse in the spur of the moment. As soon as she finished with Mrs. Baker, she had an hour break before her next appointment would arrive. Brighton most likely knew people—people who could be potential new clients. And she could always use more money.

Merri looked at her watch. "I'll have a few minutes free after I finish up with her." She nodded to the chair where Mrs. Baker sat.

"Great. I'll wait."

Brighton sat in one of the vinyl chairs in the waiting area and picked up a copy of one of the business magazines. Merri willed her heart to stop pounding as she returned to Mrs. Baker. The tiny woman had so little hair left, it didn't take long to finish the job.

Merri sensed someone watching her as she swept the hair from the floor. She looked up and met Paige's eyes. "Who is that?" Paige mouthed. "Do you know him already?"

"Later," Merri mouthed back. She and Paige were roommates while working their way through beauty school. When the opportunity to open *The Cut* presented itself, Merri knew Paige would be a good addition. Her styling skills were great and customers loved her. Unfortunately, she also felt it was her mission in life to play matchmaker for Merri.

Finished sweeping, Merri dumped the discarded hair into the trash and stepped to the waiting area. "I can help you now," she told Brighton. *You're doing*

4

good, Merri. Just keep the conversation to a minimum and you'll get through this.

He followed her to the sink area where she instructed him to sit. "I always do a quick wash first. Lean back."

Brighton obeyed and she sprayed his hair down with water. She hesitated before touching it, though. Washing other people's hair was something she did all day long, but the idea of touching Brighton Stansbury's hair seemed oddly intimate...and not in a good way.

She took a deep breath and plunged her hands in. The sooner she got it over with, the sooner she could get him out of her salon.

"Have you been in Salt Lake since high school?" he asked as she wrapped a towel around his head after all the shampoo had been rinsed.

"Yes." *Good job, Merri. Short and sweet.*

"Do you see a lot of people from our graduating class? I haven't been back for a long time. I wonder about some of them."

"Occasionally."

Their eyes met in the large mirror over her supply table and Merri quickly looked away. "How short do you want it?"

"Not too short. I mostly just need a touch up around my ears and in the back."

Merri picked up her electric clippers and looked from them to the back of Brighton's head. It wouldn't be too hard to claim the safety slipped off. A bald patch in the back of his head would grow back in— eventually. If she were still in high school, she wouldn't have thought twice about it. Brighton Stansbury's hair would have been destroyed in a matter of seconds. But now she had a business and a reputation to think about. Not to mention the fact that at her age she should be more mature.

She kept the attachment on the clippers and went to work on his hair, staying mostly quiet. Usually she chatted with her customers and enjoyed getting to know them, but having Brighton in the same room as her for the first time in seven years made her tense. She didn't have any idea what to say to him.

"So...are you married? Any kids?" he asked.

"Not yet." She shook her head, knowing he could see her in the mirror, and then stole a glance at his left hand. No ring on his ring finger. "How about you?" she asked anyway.

Brighton chuckled. "Not even close."

"I'm not surprised." The words slipped out before she could stop them. Embarrassed by her own lack of maturity, she turned so her back was to him in the mirror.

"What's that supposed to mean?" he asked.

There's no way out of this conversation. "I didn't think you were the type to settle down with one girl."

"So you're saying I'm a player?"

"Your word, not mine." She clipped the last lock and turned back to the mirror.

Brighton looked back at her with narrowed eyes and a half smile. "High school was a long time ago, Merri."

"I know. It's nice that we could all move on."

Brighton nodded and rose from his chair. "How much do I owe you?"

"I'll ring you up at the cash register." She walked back to the front of the salon, noticing that he stopped to stuff money into her tip jar before following. The thought of Brighton Stansbury tipping her made her seethe inside. She prided herself in her ability to provide for herself and didn't want any of that money coming from the Stansburys' bottomless coffers.

"Thanks," Brighton said before stepping out the door. "I'll be back when I need another trim."

Merri watched as he shut the door, and continued to stare as he climbed into his flashy car and drove away. She didn't feel like she could fully breathe until his car completely disappeared from sight.

From across the room, Paige cleared her throat. "So...who was that?"

Merri jumped at the sudden sound, forgetting she wasn't alone in the salon. "Who was who?"

"Don't act like you don't know. The hottest guy I've ever seen in my entire life just left the salon, and he called you by name."

Merri refused to turn around, pretending to busy herself with dusting the cash register. "He's just a guy I went to school with—a really, really long time ago."

"I think he's into you."

"He's not. Trust me."

"He said he'll be back."

"Yes, when he needs another haircut." Merri finally turned around and pointed to the large sign with the salon's name hanging from the ceiling. "That's what we do here. Remember?"

Paige crossed the room and put her hands on Merri's shoulders. "I saw the way he smiled at you. If a hot guy like that smiled at me, I would have melted into a puddle right here. And then I would have attached myself to him. He'd be taking me with him even if I had to grab him around the ankles and be dragged out of here."

"I guess it's a good thing hot guys don't smile at you then. That kind of odd behavior would be bad for business."

"I'm sorry to tell you this, but you need to date more. That's a fact we both know," Paige said. "That guy that just walked out of here admitted to you that he was single and you didn't encourage him. What gives?"

Merri sighed. "First of all, I've known him almost my entire life. The two of us don't get along—like, at all—so he'd never ask me out. Second of all, if he somehow lost his mind and *did* ask me out, I'd say no. I don't care for self-absorbed rich boys like Brighton Stansbury."

Paige's mouth dropped open and a mini scream escaped. "Wait...did you just say Stansbury? As in the richest family in all of Utah?"

"That's the one."

"Merri! Please, please, please introduce me the next time he comes in. You might not be interested, but I am. I'll gladly cut his hair. Heck, I'll even cut his dog's hair." Paige closed her eyes. "I can just imagine running my fingers through—"

"Paige!" Merri snapped her fingers. "He won't be back. Now that he knows I'm the owner, I'm sure he'll find another place to go. And trust me, we're better off for it."

"He seemed nice enough to me."

"You know nothing about him."

"I know he's hot and he has a lot of money." Paige grinned. "What else is important?"

Merri rolled her eyes. "Trust me. He's not as nice as he seems. In eighth grade, he glued my locker door shut. It took me so long to get it open, I missed an important science test and ended up coming in second in the class for grades. Guess who was first."

Paige crossed her arms over her chest. "So—"

Merri cut her off. "In fourth grade, he told everyone I had lice, which I didn't, but everyone believed him and no one would sit by me at lunch for a month."

Paige tried to stifle a laugh. "Sounds like childish pranks."

Merri shook her head. "Don't even get me started on high school. He did everything in his power to make my life miserable. He was my competition for everything and he *always* won. And then there was his dating life. I think I'm the only girl in the entire school who didn't hook up with him at some point."

"Ahh...I see what the problem is. You don't like him because he didn't ask you out back then."

Merri's jaw dropped. "No! I take pride in the fact that I didn't follow the crowd. He's evil, Paige. Pure evil."

"Okay...umm...Merri? You need to take a breath." Paige put her hands on Merri's shoulders. "I think you're about to hyperventilate. And you're talking like a crazy person. This isn't like you."

Merri took a deep breath. "He always brings out the worst in me. You'd be doing yourself a favor to stay away from him."

Paige shrugged. "People can change. Just think, if I can score a date with that guy, it might lead to a second date. Second dates can lead to third dates, which can lead to marriage, and that family is definitely one I'd marry into."

"I think you're getting a little ahead of yourself."

Paige grinned. "Whatever you say."

Merri turned to face Paige and crossed her arms over her chest. "What's that supposed to mean?"

"What?"

"Your smile...and your tone."

Paige took a step back, putting distance between herself and Merri. "I'm just saying, you reacted to him."

"Yes. I reacted by hiding under a chair, remember?"

"You blushed, you twisted your finger through your hair, and you leaned toward him at one point. Where I come from, that's called flirting."

Merri put her hands on her hips. "I did not do those things!"

"Check the security footage."

"We don't have video surveillance here."

"You should. There are all kinds of crazies walking around at night."

The front door of *The Cut* opened and a woman with a baby stroller in tow stepped in. "Do you have room for any walk-ins this afternoon?" she asked.

Chapter 2

Merri stood outside her sister's front door after work that evening. The smell of cinnamon permeated the air even through the thick wooden door. Nicole loved cinnamon: little red cinnamon candies, cinnamon potpourri, cinnamon candles, cinnamon bears, cinnamon on oatmeal and applesauce...even her go-to perfume carried a hint of the aroma. Whenever Merri smelled the spice, she thought fondly of her sister.

Yet, she hesitated at the door.

Typically, she would walk in unannounced and make herself at home. But that night was different. The holiday season made it that way. Nicole had invited her to the school play of her six-year-old twins, Maggie and Micah. It was a completely innocent request. After all, Merri had attended all their important events over the years and thoroughly enjoyed them. She'd sat on the sidelines and cheered as they scored their first soccer goals—although, technically, Maggie accidentally scored for the other team—and attended their graduation from Kindergarten the previous spring. She'd babysat them and played with them and read to them and their little brother Gabe countless times. And that was the problem. She loved Nicole's kids more than anything, but they weren't hers. Lately, spending time with Nicole's family only reminded her that she didn't have one of her own.

Did she want to have kids of her own? Absolutely. Did she want to have a husband who kissed her when he came home every night and asked about her day? Absolutely. Did she want a cute little home with a snowman out front surrounded by little boot prints? Absolutely. Did she have any of those things? Nope. Not even close.

Taking a deep breath, Merri turned the door handle and pushed her way into the home.

"Merri!" Maggie saw her immediately and skidded across the entranceway tile to give her a hug. Floppy reindeer ears protruded from her niece's golden hair and a red-painted nose accented her face.

"Whoa. Careful there, Rudolph. Your nose might not look so good if you rubbed it off on my white sweater." Merri laughed as she bent to give Maggie a hug, carefully avoiding the red paint.

Maggie stomped her foot. "I'm not Rudolph. I'm *Rosie* the Reindeer."

"Oh, I'm so sorry." Merri pretended to be shocked. "Your costume is so great I thought you were Micah under all that paint."

Maggie grinned. "Micah's not a reindeer like me. He's mad 'cause he doesn't like his costume."

"Why doesn't he like it?"

Maggie didn't say anything but turned and pointed toward the living room. Micah sat on the couch with his arms crossed in front of his chest and his lips stuck out in a full pout. Green butcher paper wrapped around his little body from head to foot. Nicole had even painted every inch of his face green. Merri recognized the shade of paint as the same one Maggie used when she'd dressed as a witch on Halloween.

Merri chewed on her lip, trying to hold back the laugh threatening to escape. "Hey Micah, I think you look great. Are you an...elf?"

"He's a tree," Maggie whispered.

I'm striking out all over the place tonight. "I'm joking. I think you're the best looking tree in the entire state."

Micah still refused to look her way or even move so Merri followed the sound of dishes clinking together into the kitchen.

"Hey, sis," Nicole said. Her light brown hair was pulled into a sloppy ponytail and she wore an apron with something red mushed on the front, but even with all of that, Merri couldn't help but smile at Nicole's natural beauty and charm. She'd always admired her sister's ability to let life happen. "I've just got to fill a sippy cup and gather snacks for Gabe and then we can leave. Paul called. He's stuck in traffic on the freeway so he's just going to meet us at the school."

"Can I do anything to help?" Merri asked.

"Not unless you can convince Micah that he'll be the star of the show."

"I already tried. And I failed miserably."

Maggie reappeared just then. "Mom! Gabe did it again."

13

Nicole's eyes widened. "Did what?"

"You know, that thing you get really mad about."

Nicole rubbed the back of her hand across her forehead. "Please tell me you're joking."

"Uh uh. Come see."

Merri put up a hand to stop her sister. "I've got this. You just finish whatever you need to get ready in here." Merri didn't know what to expect as she followed Maggie down the hall and when she found it, she regretted being in such a hurry to offer help.

"See," Maggie said, pointing into the little bathroom between the boys' room and Maggie's room.

"Me did it," two-year-old Gabe said proudly as he pointed toward the toilet. Merri stepped cautiously into the room and peered over the edge of the porcelain bowl. An entire roll of toilet paper—even the cardboard tubing—floated in the water. Three superhero action figures bobbed up and down amid the mass of sludge.

Merri took a deep breath. "Gabe, this is naughty. Never put things in the toilet, okay?"

Gabe just grinned back. He had a shock of blonde hair that Nicole refused to let Merri cut no matter how much she begged—something about not being ready for her baby to look grown up with a real haircut.

Merri pushed up the sleeves of her sweater and leaned over the toilet bowl. "Maggie, can you pass the trash can this way?"

Maggie scooted the can toward Merri with her foot. "You're not going to stick your hand in there, are you?"

"How else are we going to get it all out?"

"Like this." Maggie reached her hand toward the

14

toilet handle.

"No!" Merri cried. She lunged for Maggie's hand but didn't get there in time. Instead, she found herself jumping back as the soupy toilet water began to bubble over the edge of the bowl.

Maggie frowned. "Oops."

Merri took a deep breath and smiled. "It's okay. We can clean this up, too. Just find me some towels."

Nicole appeared in the doorway just as Merri finished cleaning up the mess and tossing the last of the action figures into their hot tub—aka sink full of water and disinfectant. "I'm so sorry you had to clean this up. I thought Gabe outgrew the habit of putting everything in there."

"Apparently not." Merri laughed. "It's not a big deal. We took care of it."

"Just add it to the giant list of things I owe you for. We better go or we're going to be late."

The twins attended Mountain Peak Elementary about a mile away. By the time their group arrived, the small auditorium was almost full. Luckily, Nicole's husband Paul beat them to the school and managed to save a few seats in the middle.

"Aren't they so cute up there?" Nicole gushed as the class paraded onto the stage. "I can't believe they're mine."

Merri smiled. "You're a lucky woman."

Nicole turned to her and whispered, "Sorry. What about you? Any news in the romance department these days?"

For some reason her mind immediately drifted to Brighton Stansbury. She shuddered and pushed the thought away. "Nope. Nothing."

"You know, Paul works with this guy. I could set

you up if you want. He's really nice, but—"

"Stop right there. Anytime there's a 'but' involved, I know I'm not going to be interested. I don't want a guy I have to settle for."

"Got it." Nicole looped her arm through Merri's and they both returned their attention to the stage.

A few of the other students were dressed just like Maggie, with antlers and red noses. They pranced around while the rest of the class sang a silly song about Santa's helpers. Midway through the class's fourth song, Merri's phone vibrated in her pocket. She pulled it out and glanced at the number. Unknown. Knowing that the phone for *The Cut* transferred all incoming calls to her cell during non-business hours, she quickly stepped into the hall to answer it.

"Hello?"

"*Merri?*"

"Yes."

"*This is Brighton.*"

Twice in one day. Did the universe hate her? "Can I help you with something?"

"*I'm looking for someone to cut my Nana's hair. She likes a fresh cut and style for every holiday. She's ninety and doesn't have much else to excite her, you know what I mean?*"

"Uh huh."

"*Anyway, Nana's hairstylist retired recently and now that I know of your great new place, I thought I'd bring her to you.*"

"That's fine. What day would you like?"

"*Do you have any openings tomorrow?*"

"Hmm...let me see..." Merri paused, mentally flipping through the appointment book she left on the counter at the salon. This time of year, people were busy with holiday and family events. Business was slow, but Brighton didn't need to know that. "I can probably squeeze her in around 11:30."

"*That's perfect. I can take her out for lunch after you're done.*" Brighton paused. "*You're welcome to join us.*"

Merri's mouth moved, but no words came out. *Is he asking me out or just being polite? Brighton's not polite. But then, I don't think he'd ever ask me out, either.* "Thanks, but I can't leave the salon. I've got other appointments."

"*Well, maybe some other time. I'll see you tomorrow at 11:30.*"

"Great. I'll see you then."

By the time Merri returned to her seat in the auditorium, Micah stood front and center on the stage. All the other kids circled him, singing a song about trees, while they hung paper ornaments on his outstretched arms. *No wonder he didn't want to be the tree.*

"Who was on the phone?" Nicole whispered. "A hot guy maybe? You're not holding back on me are you?"

Merri hesitated. Nicole knew about her rocky past with Brighton. As far as she knew, Nicole shared her disdain for the spoiled rich boy. "Brighton Stansbury," Merri finally mumbled.

Nicole's jaw dropped. "Since when have you been hanging out with him?"

Merri quickly shook her head. "I'm not hanging out with him. He just happened to come into the salon today not knowing that I owned it. He was calling just now to set up an appointment for me to cut his grandma's hair."

Nicole twisted in her seat until she faced Merri. "When are the two of you going to stop pretending you hate each other and go on a real date?"

Merri's jaw dropped. "*Excuse me?*"

"I'm just saying, everyone was surprised when you guys made it out of high school without becoming a couple."

"Why would I have dated him? I'm proud that I'm one of the few girls who made it out of high school without going out with him. He went through girls faster than your two-year-old goes through toilet paper. Did you know that he took *two* girls to the senior prom?"

"Shh!" a lady in the row behind them hissed.

Merri and Nicole turned back to the stage, both stifling giggles. The twins once again caught Nicole's attention, but Merri couldn't focus on the presentation. Nicole said that *everyone* was surprised. Was her relationship with Brighton really the topic of conversations in high school? It didn't make sense. She couldn't stand him and everyone knew it. Didn't they?

Merri turned the key in the lock to her small apartment. It wasn't a nice big family home like Nicole's, but that didn't matter. Everything in the apartment came from her own hard work, and she couldn't be more proud of herself. When she opened *The Cut,* she moved into the apartment alone—her first time not having roommates—and began amassing furniture and decor. Sometimes the idea of going home to solitude made her happy, other times it smothered her.

She kicked off her shoes and set a takeout container on the end table next to her couch. Nicole had invited her to stay for dinner after the play, but she bowed out. Instead she opted to eat greasy diner food by herself while she watched a cheesy romance movie she rented from the machine on the corner by her apartment complex.

After the first month of living alone, Merri decided to get a pet. Birds were too noisy, dogs weren't allowed, and hamsters creeped her out. At the pet store, a furry white kitten caught her attention immediately. She had it in her arms, ready to make the leap to pet ownership, when a couple of teenagers gazing inside the lizard cage started talking about the crazy cat lady in their neighborhood. No matter how cliché it might be, she didn't want to fall into a stereotype. She went home with a couple of goldfish instead.

Merri sprinkled a pinch of fish food over the bowl on her kitchen table. "Here you go, Bomber and Betsy." She'd let each of the twins name a fish. They insisted the names needed to start with the same letter, like theirs. "How was your day? Yes, I'm talking out loud to a couple of fish. Don't judge me. You'd do the same thing if you were in my shoes."

She sat down in front of her TV and kicked her shoes off before putting her legs up on the coffee table. *Something in my life has got to change. I love my job, but I need a change of...something.*

The movie followed worn out plot lines and the ending was so predictable, Merri knew what would happen before all the characters were even introduced. She started to drift off to sleep, but a knock on the door brought her fully awake. She peered through the peephole. When she saw who stood there she sighed and closed her eyes, dropping her head against the door. Maybe if she stood there long enough, he'd go away and leave her to wallow in her misery alone. Or, he'd keep knocking.

Giving in, Merri answered the door. "Hi, Shawn."

"Hi, Merri." He didn't quite look her in the eyes. He never did. Shawn lived across the hall and appeared frequently. As far as looks go, his weren't bad. But his shyness made it hard to carry on an entire conversation.

"Can I help you with something?" Merri asked.

"Just wanted to wish you a Merry Christmas. I know it's early, but I didn't want to bother you too close to the holiday. You know, in case you were with your family. And I wouldn't want to bother you on Christmas day either. That's why I came over tonight. Actually, you're probably busy right now. Maybe I shouldn't have come. I should probably go. Sorry to bother you."

Shawn turned to return to his apartment but Merri stopped him. "Wait! You're not bothering me. Thanks for thinking of me. Merry Christmas to you, too." She still stood with one arm on the door.

Shawn looked past her into the living room. "You watching a movie?"

Merri dropped her arm. "Do you want to watch it with me?" She knew he'd never say yes.

Shawn's mouth dropped open. "Oh no. No. I wouldn't want to intrude. I'm sure you're enjoying it all by yourself in there. I just wanted to say Merry Christmas. That's all."

"I'll see you after the holidays then. Okay?"

Shawn nodded, uttered a goodbye and returned to his apartment across the hall. Merri shut the door and put on the chain and deadbolt. The poor guy found an excuse to come over at least twice a week, but he would never come in. A couple of times, Merri thought he might actually ask her out, but he never did. "What do you think, Bomber and Betsy? Should I put the guy out of his misery and ask him out myself? He's nice enough. And he's not bad looking. He's just so shy." Merri stared at the fish as if waiting for a response. "Would that be considered settling? I promised myself I would never settle."

She returned to the living room and clicked off the TV without finishing the movie, wondering when it would be her turn to have one of the romantic-comedy kind of romances. When would a movie be made about *her* troubles with love? Maybe there would never be a turn for her. She should just give in and become a cat lady. She could start with one on a trial basis. Or maybe three.

Chapter 3

Merri pulled her yellow curtains aside and looked out her bedroom window as soon as she woke, just like she did every morning. The bright curtains matched her usually sunny personality, but lately they seemed to be in opposition. She didn't know whether to blame it on the winter blues or what, but she knew one thing for sure—she'd fallen into a funk. "If I can just make it through the holidays, I won't have everyone else's happiness constantly stuffed in my face and my mood will be better," she whispered to herself.

The view from her fifth story apartment looked out over the Salt Lake Valley, the place she'd spent her entire life. She couldn't imagine living anywhere else. Her parents recently retired and bought a second home in the southern city of St. George...where it was warm. They planned to spend winters in St. George and summers in Salt Lake. Not wanting to close the salon to join them in St. George, this would be Merri's first Christmas without them. She still had Nicole's family, but it wouldn't be the same.

As she stared out the window, the clouds thickened. Fluffy white snowflakes began to fall, swirling one by one to the sidewalk below. She wished her window opened so she could stick her tongue out and catch snowflakes on it, just like she did as a child. The city already had a layer of snow from a previous storm, but the endless stream of cars and snowplows and pedestrians churning it up left it with a layer of black scum. A fresh powder would be nice for the holiday.

Merri dropped the curtain back into place and crossed her bedroom floor to her small bathroom. She turned the shower on to heat up while she chose her clothes for the day. "What to wear? What to wear?" she muttered as she looked through her closet.

She pulled out four different pairs of pants and six shirts, humming and hawing over each choice. She didn't know why she was so indecisive that morning. As soon as she got to *The Cut* she'd be covering up her carefully chosen outfit with a smock anyway. Finally deciding on a long red and gold sweater that looked great with her new skinny jeans and fur-topped winter boots, she jumped in the shower, letting the hot water wash away her funky mood. After blow drying her hair, she spent extra time curling it.

She convinced herself that the day warranted extra attention since it was the last day *The Cut* would be open before Christmas. It couldn't possibly have anything to do with the fact that Brighton Stansbury would be coming in with his Nana.

Having spent extra time on her appearance, Merri didn't have much time for breakfast. Instead of her usual oatmeal with sliced bananas, she grabbed an apple off the counter on her way out the door. The chilly air surprised her, taking her breath away. The snowflakes were coming down en masse by that point and it took ten minutes to clear the accumulated layers of snow and ice from her windows before she could pull out of the parking lot of her apartment complex. Getting to *The Cut* took extra time because of the slick roads and jammed traffic. By the time she unlocked the front door to her salon, she was already five minutes late. *Totally unacceptable.*

Paige stood under the eaves of the building, holding an umbrella over her head. She lived two blocks away and walked to work every morning. In the few months *The Cut* had been open, that day was the first time Paige beat Merri to work.

"I thought maybe I'd gotten mixed up and you weren't opening today," Paige said.

"Sorry. It's just one thing after another these days. I think the world is out to get me."

"I hear ya, sister. How many appointments do you have scheduled today?"

Merri stomped her boots on the entryway mat and hung her coat behind her station before checking the appointment book. "Only a few for me and a couple for you. I'm hoping we get a lot of walk-ins." Merri picked up a pen and wrote Brighton Stansbury's name in the book.

Paige leaned over her shoulder, watching her write. "Wait...Brighton Stansbury? As in yesterday's hottie?"

Merri gave one small nod, but didn't meet Paige's eyes.

"He's coming again already? That must have been some haircut you gave him." Paige walked to the other side of the counter, humming a cheesy love song.

"It's not what you think. He called last night to see if I could fit his grandma in this morning. I'm not even sure if he's coming with her." *Although he sort of invited me to lunch with them, so...*

"Be warned, now that I know who he is, I'm not going to hold back. He's going to be my Christmas present this year." Paige paused. "Unless of course you've changed your mind about him."

Merri smiled. "Be my guest. Just don't bring him around here any more than necessary."

"Deal."

They worked side by side, getting the salon ready for the day. Merri plugged in the lights on a Christmas tree she'd splurged on for the waiting room and set a bowl of miniature candy canes next to the cash register.

"You know, I've been thinking," Paige began after a few moments of silence. "If I'm going to be the next Mrs. Stansbury, it would only be fair to find someone for you, too. I'd hate to come in here every day glowing in happiness if you were still single. I mean, what kind of a friend would I be if I did that?"

"I'm not sure I like where this conversation is heading," Merri said, not happy that Brighton Stansbury had come up yet again.

"Well, I was thinking, have I ever told you about my cousin Harrison?"

Merri closed her eyes and took a deep breath. "Harrison that's thirty-seven and still working on his first bachelor degree?"

"So I *have* mentioned him then."

"Yes. And every time his name comes up it's because you're complaining about something stupid he's done."

"Really? That doesn't sound right. He's not that bad. And even though he's my cousin, I'm willing to admit that he's kind of cute."

Merri sighed, but let Paige continue.

"Anyway, I was thinking—"

"Paige?" Merri interrupted.

"Yeah?"

"There's no way I'm going out with your cousin. Got it? I don't know how I'm going to do it, but I'm going to find my perfect match by myself. Thanks for your concern, but you don't need to be my matchmaker."

"Got it."

The morning passed slowly. Merri gave two quick haircuts just after they opened and then sat in one of the salon chairs with her feet up reading the latest gossip magazines the salon had subscriptions to while Paige finished a cut and color. The more often she looked at the time, the slower it seemed to move. Finally, at exactly 11:30, the bell above the door rang. She jumped from the chair and tossed the magazine onto the chair cushion as Brighton stepped up to the counter.

"Good morning," he said.

"Hi." Merri looked behind him. "I think you forgot something."

Brighton turned. "Really? What?"

"Uh...your Nana? Go ahead and bring her in while I get the chair ready." Merri started to turn away, but Brighton reached out and grabbed her arm. It felt like a zap of electricity coursed through her body.

"Hold on," he said.

Brighton saw the look of alarm on her face as she stared at his hand on her arm and quickly let go. "I didn't actually bring her with me."

Merri raised her eyebrows. "You want me to cut her hair by using my mind? Even I'm not that good."

"I'll give it a try," Paige called from across the room. "I learned some pretty cool tricks while in beauty school."

Merri glared at her.

Brighton smiled his famous half-grin and focused his attention on Merri. She knew that grin well. He plastered it on his face every time he wanted to get his way. For some reason, it made Merri blush and she quickly looked down, shuffling through the stack of receipts by the register. "Yeah, about Nana. She decided she doesn't want to come out in this storm. Have you been outside today? It's getting crazy out there."

Merri glanced over his shoulder. The snow hadn't let up and was coming down even harder than when she first got to work. She'd heard snowplows go back and forth in front of the salon all morning, but they struggled to keep up with the amount of snow being dumped. "You could have called. You didn't need to come all the way over here in this storm just to cancel an appointment."

"I don't live that far from here. It's not a big deal. Besides, I have a proposal for you."

Merri tilted her head and put one hand on her hip. "A proposal? Guys usually take me out at least once before they propose." *Oh my gosh! I can't believe I just said that! Paige was right. I do sound like I'm flirting with him!*

Brighton chuckled. "Did I mention before that Nana is ninety-years-old? Leaving her house to do anything can be a struggle. She's becoming quite the homebody. I thought maybe you could make a home visit. You know, cut her hair in the comfort of her own home."

Merri started to shake her head and opened her mouth to say no, but Brighton cut her off before any sound came out.

"I'll pay you extra for a home visit, of course."

Merri narrowed her eyes. "I'm not a charity case."

Brighton looked shocked. "I didn't mean it like that. I swear. I just…"

"There's no way I can leave the building. I've got clients coming and Paige is leaving early tonight so I'll have to close up."

"By the way, my plans changed. I can close for you if you want," Paige called from across the room, her eyes and grin focused on Brighton.

Merri turned around and glared at her again. "I couldn't do that to you. Not so close to Christmas."

"Yes you could. I won't mind at all." Paige winked.

Merri gritted her teeth and turned back to Brighton.

"It doesn't have to be right this minute," he said. "You can go up there after you've finished your appointments."

"Up there?"

"She lives up the canyon. It's kind of secluded."

"I guess the answer is no then. I don't have snow tires on my car. It would never make it on these roads."

"I can drive you up there. It's kind of hard to find anyway. We'll be back by early evening."

Merri looked over his shoulder and eyed his sports car parked on the street by the front window. "You think that little thing will make it up the canyon in this weather?"

Brighton followed Merri's eyes to his parked car. His own eyes sparkled. "No way. I've got an SUV, too. I'll go trade before we leave."

Of course you own more than one vehicle. "You're sure this Nana of yours is real? You're not just trying to get me in your car so you can leave me stranded out in the west desert somewhere are you?"

"Come on, are you still mad about that time my friends and I made you and Hailey walk home from the Spirit Club field trip?"

"It was five miles of desert! And it was really, really cold."

"It was sixty degrees and I doubt it was more than two miles."

"Sixty degrees *is* cold."

"No, *that's* cold," Brighton said as he pointed outside. "What do you say? Are you in?"

Truthfully, she had plans. She'd agreed to go to Nicole's house for once-a-year Christmas entertainment as soon as she got off work. They'd sing carols, act out the nativity, and the kids would attempt to open their gifts early—exactly like every other year. It would be a perfectly fine evening. Or, she could live dangerously and try something new. Of course, something new would require her to spend time in an enclosed vehicle with Brighton Stansbury. The choice was a tossup.

"*Please?*" Brighton begged. "You'll make Nana's Christmas perfect."

Merri tapped her red-nailed fingers on the

counter. "Fine." She sighed loudly for effect and turned her back to him. "I'll do it. Come back at three."

"Thanks. I'm looking forward to this. And I'll owe you one after this trip so be thinking of what you want me to do for repayment."

She whirled around, surprised at Brighton's words, but he'd already stepped out the door.

Chapter 4

"Where exactly is your Nana's house?" Merri asked after tucking a duffel bag full of hair supplies into the backseat of Brighton's black SUV a few hours later.

"Big Cottonwood Canyon."

Merri glanced nervously out the window at the accumulating snow. Even though she'd lived through twenty-five Utah winters, she still got nervous at the thought of driving on snow-covered roads. "Maybe we should wait until after Christmas to do this. I can go up this weekend if you want. I don't have plans and the salon will be closed on Saturday."

Brighton shook his head. "I can't do that to her. Nana loves looking her best for Christmas and in her ninety-year-old mind, that includes getting her hair done. I promised her. And I don't break my promises."

Merri folded her hands tightly in her lap and leaned back in her seat, wondering if she dared close her eyes for the remainder of the trip. It would all be over in a couple of hours.

"So...you like to cut hair?" Brighton asked after they'd driven in silence for a few minutes.

"Did you figure that one out all by yourself?" she teased.

"Okay. I'll give you that one."

"Yes. I like cutting hair."

"How long have you been doing it?"

"I got my cosmetology license right after high school and then worked during the days and went to school in the evening until I earned my business degree. It might not be an ultra fancy salon, but I earned every penny of it and paid for all the hard work of building up to it. Not all of us could afford to go to college without working." Merri immediately regretted her last sentence, but it was too late to take it back. She looked out the window, unwilling to meet the stare she felt Brighton giving her.

"What did I ever do to make you hate me so much?" Brighton finally said, amusement in his voice.

Merri forced herself to look at him. "What *didn't* you do?"

"Excuse me?"

"You've been harassing me since the day we met."

"In what way?"

"You pulled my hair."

Brighton laughed out loud. "Seriously? You're still mad about that? Come on, Merri. We were six years old. Let it go."

"In second grade, you broke the tips off all my brand new crayons. I couldn't seem to color inside the lines the rest of the school year."

"I only did that because you put snow inside my backpack. It melted all over my homework and I ended up having to redo everything."

32

"Fine. In fifth grade, you let the air out of my bike tires and I had to push my bike home."

"Maybe I did start that one, but you retaliated by telling the principal that I was the one that overflowed all the toilets in the teacher's lounge." Brighton laughed. "I'd never even been in that room."

Before she could stop it, a short laugh escaped her throat. Merri had forgotten all about the incident with the teacher's lounge. At the time, she didn't know for sure if Brighton had executed the prank, but she figured he deserved to be punished for something...so she ratted him out.

Brighton gasped. "It's a Christmas miracle. I got Merri Wilcox to smile."

Merri quickly turned away again, chiding herself for showing weakness. "And then there was the time in junior high when you beat me in the school spelling bee."

"Why would you bring that up? I won that fair and square. I studied for the spelling bee every night for a month. I think I even spelled a few words in my sleep."

"I studied hard, too. I didn't do anything after school except study spelling words for *two* months. I knew you would be my biggest competition."

Brighton glanced at her. "I'm not sure what to say to this. Did you want me to drop out or misspell words on purpose? Would it have been a satisfying victory if you knew I purposely lost?"

Merri lifted her shoulders and dropped them again. "What about our senior year when we ran against each other to be student body president? I bet I would have won if it wasn't for the fact that you had all of your daddy's money to bribe votes with and all I had was the pathetic babysitting money I'd saved all summer. You handed out gift certificates to the ice cream parlor and all I could afford to hand out was Tootsie Rolls." She stopped talking to catch her breath. "You *always* won. You'd think I would have thought of that before I even bothered running for office. And you know what? Losing was one thing, but sending your friends to rub your win in my face? That was just low." Merri folded her arms over her chest and set her jaw. *I hate that he brings out the worst in me. I'd never talk to anyone else this way. I'm awful.*

The windshield wipers thumped each time they went back and forth as they fought to clear the snow. No other sound could be heard as silence filled the car. They'd entered the canyon and could barely see through the driving snow. She couldn't remember the last time a car had passed by on the other side of the highway. Apparently no one else was stupid enough to try driving up the canyon in the storm.

Merri peeked at Brighton from the corner of her eyes. His lips were turned down in a frown, and Merri felt her heart sink. Watching Brighton accomplish all of his dreams while she spent her life fighting for everything and still coming up short had left her bitter. Her school days were long behind her and she needed to let the past go. Not everything that had gone wrong in her life had been Brighton's fault. Maybe she could cut him a little slack for a few hours.

She took a deep breath, gearing up to apologize, and turned her head toward Brighton. "Look out!" Merri screamed as a deer bounded from behind the trees on the side of the road and out in front of the SUV.

Brighton threw his arm out protectively as he

34

braked hard and cranked the steering wheel, trying to avoid a collision with the animal. The tires squealed as they struggled to grip the icy roads. Despite his best efforts to stop it, the SUV spun out of control before careening off the side of the road. Merri closed her eyes, not wanting to see what fate awaited them. They came to a jerking stop and she opened her eyes again. Their vehicle had come to a stop at the bottom of a powdery slope.

Brighton breathed hard. "Are you okay?" His arm still pressed against Merri as he searched her face for a genuine response.

Even though her heart felt like it might pound a hole through her chest and her stomach threatened to give up the contents of the lunch she'd eaten behind the counter of *The Cut*, Merri managed to nod her head. "I'm fine."

"I swear that deer came out of nowhere. I wasn't even going that fast because of the roads. I think we missed him though." Brighton peered over the windshield and out his side window.

"I think you're right. We would have felt it if we hit him."

Brighton glanced out his window again. "I'm going to see what the chances are of digging ourselves out of this mess." He shoved against his door, but it wouldn't open more than a couple of inches. With each push of his shoulder against the door, the SUV rocked back and forth, but he didn't make any progress. "Try your door," he instructed Merri.

She pulled on the handle and then shoved against the door. Her side of the car opened even less than Brighton's. Panic started to set in as she realized that one of her worst nightmares—being trapped with

35

Brighton Stansbury—might become a reality. "We can't get out. What are we going to do? No one will find us down here until Spring!"

Brighton placed a comforting hand on her shoulder. "It'll be okay. I'll climb over the seat and see if the back doors open. We'll get out. I promise."

Merri took a deep breath and closed her eyes, willing her body to calm down. She turned in her seat as the SUV began to rock again with Brighton's efforts to get the back doors open. Still no success.

"I'll try the hatch in the back. If that doesn't work, we might have to crawl out a window," Brighton called over the back of the seat. "Can you pull the lever to pop the hatch? It's by the driver's side door."

Merri climbed over the middle console and felt around until she found the lever. "Got it!" she called as she pulled on it.

Much to her relief, and probably Brighton's, the hatch slowly lifted and they were greeted by a blast of cold air and snow. "I've got a small shovel back here," Brighton said. "I'm going to assess our situation and then I'll be back."

He slammed the hatch closed as he left and Merri suddenly felt very alone—and very trapped. Until that moment, she didn't know she had claustrophobia. She turned her head, trying to keep Brighton's green and orange coat in her sight at all times. She periodically heard faint scraping sounds as he made valiant attempts to dig the car out of the snow. Ten minutes later, he pounded on the hatch and she popped it open again.

"Any luck?" she asked as he climbed into the cargo area and pulled the hatch closed behind himself.

Brighton shook the snow from his coat before

answering. He looked funny scrunched inside the cargo area. "There's no way we're getting out of this drift by ourselves. I'm really sorry. I shouldn't have pressured you into coming with me. This is all my fault."

"Don't worry about it. You were just trying to do something nice for your grandma."

"We'll have to call a tow truck. Whenever there's a storm, they get busy. Hopefully we can find one that can get up here. I don't want you to miss out on Christmas celebrations with your family."

Merri laughed. "It won't be the end of the world if I miss it. I'm not exactly looking forward to it."

Brighton raised his eyebrows. "I've met your parents. They seemed nice enough."

"My parents are great, but they moved to St. George for the winter. I'm supposed to go over to my sister's house tonight."

"And you don't get along with her?"

"No. That's not it at all. Nicole and I get along great."

"I don't see what the problem is."

Merri wrapped her arms around herself in an attempt to stay warm. "It's just...well...the holidays are kind of a reminder that I'm the only one of my friends and family that doesn't have kids or any prospects of having any in the near future. My sister has three little kids and I adore them, but her house is somewhat of a zoo. Sometimes I feel like I'm her project. I don't want to be anyone's project." The words fell out, surprising Merri. She hadn't intended to spill her guts to Brighton. "You probably wouldn't understand."

From his perch in the cargo area, Merri saw

Brighton flash his half smile. "Trust me. I know exactly what you mean. Sounds like we're in the same situation. I can only handle so many family dinners where I'm asked when I'm going to produce heirs or why I'm not married yet. And don't get me started on people trying to set me up on blind dates."

"Blind dates! Yes! The second anyone hears I'm single, they insist they have the perfect match for me. How is someone I've just met supposed to know what my perfect match is like? It never works out. Just because two people are single doesn't mean they're perfect for each other."

"Exactly. I've managed to avoid Christmases with my family the last couple of years. I planned to spend this one with Nana. My parents are in Europe and my siblings won't miss me."

"Just so you're aware, even though I'm not excited to go to my sister's house, it doesn't mean I want to spend the night trapped in this car."

"Right." Brighton pulled his phone from his back pocket. "I'll call a tow truck." He fiddled with the phone for a few seconds before saying, "I don't have any service. That's just great. How about you?"

Merri leaned across the console and picked up her purse. She had to dig through the contents of her bag to find her phone. *Please don't let me be stuck here with Brighton Stansbury,* she chanted over and over in her head while searching.

"Any luck?" he asked when Merri hesitated.

She looked down at her screen as it powered on. "Nothing. We're trapped here."

Chapter 5

Brighton glanced out the back window of the SUV. "I think the snow's starting to let up a little. We're not that far from Nana's house now. Maybe a couple of miles away is all. And she's got a landline we can call a tow truck from. Do you want to stay here in the car and wait for me to get back or walk to her house with me?"

Merri glanced out her window at the lowering sun. No way was she staying in the car alone. "I'm coming with you."

"Are you sure?"

"Positive. The last thing I want is to be trapped in here, unable to get out, when you get lost and don't come back."

"Thanks for the confidence boost."

"No problem."

Merri pulled Brighton's keys from the ignition and tossed them to him in the back. She popped the hatch again and attempted to crawl over the seats as gracefully as possible. "They might not be thick, but I'm glad I decided to wear boots this morning. When I left my apartment, I had no idea I'd be going hiking. I guess I should have worn snowshoes instead."

"Merri, I'm so sorry about this."

"It's not your fault. It could have happened to anyone." She smiled, partially to prove her sincerity to Brighton and partially to convince herself. Before she climbed over the middle seat to the back, she grabbed the bag full of hair cutting supplies she'd brought. "I might as well cut Nana's hair while we're waiting for the tow truck."

"Good idea. After all this, we better at least do what we came for, right?" He watched as she struggled into the cargo area. "Too bad I don't have a sun roof. That would have made the exit a little easier."

Merri didn't say anything else as she slid out the back. She sank past her knees in the deep snow immediately, her boots filling with powder on the first step. She gasped as the cold, wet snow soaked through to her feet. "We're going to die out here."

"That's a real possibility," Brighton teased, flashing his perfectly straight white teeth. "I think I have a flashlight in here somewhere. It might come in handy." He popped open a compartment in the floor of the cargo area and pulled out a heavy black flashlight. He turned it on, checking for battery life. "Works great," he said as he reached up to slam the hatch closed. "Be Prepared. All my years in the Boy Scouts finally paid off."

Merri tried to take a step back to get out of the way of the descending door, but her legs still stuck in the deep snow and all she managed to do was fall backward onto her rear end. "And now you know why Grace is my middle name," Merri said wryly as she accepted Brighton's hand to pull herself up.

"I *didn't* know that. Is Grace really your middle name?"

Merri nodded. "Uh huh. Not very fitting, I know."

"I don't know, I kind of like it."

"What about you? Any middle name?" she asked.

Brighton took the bag of hair supplies from her and swung it over his shoulder. "The least I can do is carry this. You already have your purse to carry and that thing looks big. You sure you don't want to wait here with the car?"

"Positive. And why did you change the subject?"

Brighton looked at her with raised brows. "Huh?"

"Don't play dumb. I want to know what your middle name is. You know mine so it's only fair. I promise I won't tell anyone—not that I know anyone who would care."

Brighton chewed on the corner of his lip. "I don't think I've ever willingly told anyone before."

"There's a first time for everything."

"Fine, but keep in mind that my parents are a little crazy."

"Everyone's parents are a little crazy. That's no secret. And your parents must be slightly less crazy than most or they wouldn't have built such a fortune."

"My full name is Brighton Washington Jefferson Franklin Stansbury."

Merri stifled a laugh. "I don't believe you."

"I wish it weren't true. My parents—okay, my dad—wanted to name me after one of the founding fathers. Sadly, he couldn't decide which one."

"You're joking."

Brighton put one hand over his heart. "Cross my heart and hope to die."

"How long did that take you to learn as a child?"

"A lot longer than everyone with normal names."

"No offense, but that's awful."

"You should see my social security card. It takes two lines to fit all my name."

Merri couldn't control her emotions any longer and a loud laugh escaped. She quickly covered her mouth with her hand. "I'm sorry. Really. And I promise never to complain about my middle name again." She paused. "Do you have monogrammed towels? I bet BWJFS looks great embroidered in white on red terrycloth."

"Ha, ha, ha. You're hilarious. I guess I proved your theory that I win everything. I even won the battle for craziest middle name."

Merri removed her gloves for a minute while she tucked flyaway strands of hair under her hood. "That's one battle I'll gladly let you win."

Each step up the embankment to the road took a concentrated effort and they slipped more than once. "Here," Brighton said.

Merri looked up from the snow to see his hand stretched toward her. She hesitated before shrugging her shoulders and accepting his hand.

"If we want to make it back down to the valley in time to go to your sister's house, we need to hurry."

"Like I said before, it's not a big deal if I miss it." Even with her hand securely encased in a glove, the feel of his hand wrapped around hers occupied all her thoughts. Brighton maintained that grip on her hand as the pair continued the slow climb toward the road.

Whenever they made progress, they'd slide back a few feet and have to climb again. By the time they made it to the top of the slope, they were both covered in snow and struggling to catch their breath in the cold.

"I guess I won't need to work out before bed tonight," Brighton said.

"I don't think I'll need to work out the rest of the week. Or maybe I'll just treat myself to an extra bag of Christmas candy."

"I like that idea."

Merri pulled the strings of her hood as tight as she could. Only her nose and part of her eyes could be seen. The car and slope were sheltered from the wind, but the road sat fully in its path. The cold cut through them like a thousand tiny needles. "I think I got turned around when we were spinning in the car. Which way do we go from here?"

Brighton pointed down the road to his right. "That's the way to Nana's, but..."

"But?"

Brighton moved to stand next to her. "Well, it hasn't been that long since we turned onto this road. Maybe half a mile." He rubbed his hand across his chin. "We can go the shorter way back to the main road and hope that someone comes along before it gets dark, keeping in mind that it's been a while since someone passed us, or we can go this way," he pointed to his right again, "and we'll find Nana's house in a couple of miles, but probably not any cars."

Merri looked at the sun one more time. She could barely see it through the trees, but knew from the angle and amount of light coming from it that it wouldn't be long before they were in complete darkness. If they went the shorter route to the main road and a car never came by, they'd be in big trouble. "Let's go to Nana's."

"Good choice."

No snow plows had been down the road they were on in quite some time, if at all, and they left two distinct pairs of footprints as they walked—one men's size ten and one women's size seven.

"Are you warm enough?" Brighton asked.

"As warm as can be expected."

"In other words, you're freezing. Do you want my coat to wear on top of your own?"

"Nope. I have no idea where we're going. If you die from exposure, I'll be in big trouble out here by myself."

"Good point."

"It's not that bad." It wasn't a complete lie. She'd been in colder temperatures before. Of course, she'd never hiked in that kind of weather…

They walked in silence for a few minutes. It felt awkward not to converse, but speaking in the cold and wind only added to their discomfort. Finally, Brighton cleared his throat and stuffed his hands in his coat pockets. "Umm…what did you mean earlier? I mean, back when we were still in the car. You said that I sent my friends to rub my student body win in your face."

Great. We're back to that extremely awkward conversation. I'm not sure what's worse, awkward silence or awkward conversations. "I just meant that I didn't appreciate it. That's all."

"I didn't know my friends said anything to you."

Merri turned to peek at him through her hood, not sure if he was telling the truth. "Really? You didn't send them to tell me that I'd never beat you at anything and I might as well give up? Oh, and they also said, and I quote, 'Brighton said to tell you to remember that you'll always be a loser.'"

Brighton stopped walking, but Merri kept going. Finally, after getting ten paces ahead of him, she stopped and turned around. Brighton stood where he'd stopped, shaking his head."Merri, I never told anyone to say those things. I swear. I would never do that." He adjusted his hat on his head. "Tell me who it was."

"It doesn't matter now. It happened a long time ago."

"It matters if you don't believe me."

The last thing I need is to be known as a tattletale this many years after we graduated. I'm more mature than that. "I believe you," Merri lied.

"It probably doesn't mean much now, but...I think you would have made a great Student Body President. You had school spirit, you were in at least a dozen clubs, you were smart, and I'm pretty sure you knew every person in the entire school—even all the underclassmen."

"Yeah, well, like I said before...it doesn't matter now. The student body chose you."

Thankfully, Brighton changed the subject. "It's getting dark. Do you want to hold the flashlight or do you want me to?"

"I'll hold it. You're already carrying my bag."

Brighton handed the flashlight to Merri and she turned it on. In the growing darkness, all her senses were heightened. Every sound from the crunch of her boots in the snow to the flutter of a bird's wings caught her attention. She could smell the pine trees surrounding them and sucked in a long cold breath, remembering the scent that reminded her so much of childhood.

"We used to cut our own Christmas trees," she told Brighton. "Every year we'd head to Dad's favorite spot during the first weekend in December and search and search until we found the perfect tree. Mom always brought tomato soup in Thermoses. When I was fifteen or sixteen, they bought a fake tree. I miss the smell of pine needles during the holidays."

"You could try a pine-scented candle."

"I have. It's not the same. This year I bought a real pine wreath for the door of my salon. One of my customers was selling them. I can't smell it from inside, though."

"I know what you mean about the smell. My parents always get real trees, but they're usually delivered to the house. I never got to cut one down as a child. Sounds fun."

"It was."

Brighton suddenly reached out and touched her hand. "Turn off the flashlight for a minute."

She tilted her head nervously. "Why? What's wrong? Do you see something? Is it an animal?" Visions of a giant bear with razor sharp teeth running through the woods toward them flooded her mind."

When she didn't turn the flashlight off, Brighton took it from her hand and did it himself. "Nothing's wrong. Trust me."

She stopped walking.

"See." Brighton pointed through the trees. "Can you see that red glow through there?"

"A little."

"Those are the Christmas lights on Nana's house."

"We're almost there!"

"Sort of. The turn to her driveway isn't far, but her driveway is probably half a mile long."

"At least there's some light at the end of the tunnel, right?"

Brighton laughed. "You could say that."

The idea that a warm home grew ever nearer lifted her spirits. Merri surprised herself by easily chatting with Brighton as they reached the turn off. By the time Nana's house came into view, she'd almost forgotten she didn't like him.

Chapter 6

As they turned down the lane to Nana's house, the storm picked up in its intensity again and the wind came with it. Merri's hood kept blowing off in the wind and she had no choice but to pull one hand out of her pocket to hold it in place on her head. The wind whipped through her and the snow pounding against her cheeks pricked so hard, she wouldn't have been surprised to see blood. Even though she could see the faint red glow of Nana's house through the trees, she wondered if she might freeze to death before they reached it.

Brighton saw Merri struggling and wrapped an arm around her shoulders. It helped hold her hood up and kept her walking in the right direction.

"I can't tell you how awful I feel about this," Brighton yelled, trying to compete with the howling wind. "I swear I checked the weather before I left and the news said the storm would end by afternoon."

"I told you, it's fine," Merri yelled in return, still trying to convince him. Her face stayed warmer if she didn't open her mouth longer than necessary.

The remaining half mile took longer than the rest of the walk by far and when the full house finally came into view, Merri found herself quickening her pace. "It's the prettiest thing I've ever seen," she mumbled through chattering teeth.

Brighton turned to her, fighting to keep his own hood up with the hand not wrapped around her shoulders. "What was that? I can't hear you!"

"Never mind," she yelled back.

Nana's house wasn't just a house. Merri thought calling it a cabin would have been a more accurate description. Rough hewn logs made up the exterior and a wraparound porch surrounded the structure. Red Christmas lights lined the edge of the roof and real pine garlands swooped and twisted as they wrapped around the porch railing. A large holly wreath hung prominently on the front door. The scene, set in the snowy pines, reminded Merri of a Christmas card and she almost cried as she took it all in. "It's beautiful!"

"Just wait until you see the inside. I want a home just like this someday."

"I'm sure you'll get it...just like everything." *Grr. I've got to stop putting my foot in my mouth.* She turned to see Brighton's reaction, but he didn't act as if he heard the comment. *Thank you, wind.*

From the top of the one story cabin, a brick chimney billowed smoke—and the promise of warmth—into the evening air. As they forged a path up the snow-laden front steps, Merri breathed in the smoky air that reminded her of days spent in front of the wood-burning stove at her own grandparents' home as a child.

Brighton dropped his arm from Merri's shoulder and rapped firmly on the front door. They only waited a moment before a little white-haired lady opened it. Her eyebrows shot up and her hand went to her mouth in shock. "Bright! I can't believe you really came up here in this weather," she said. "I always knew you were crazy, but this is ridiculous even for you."

"I promised you I'd come up tonight. I never break my promises."

"That may be true, but maybe you should think about breaking one now and then."

Merri smiled and held back a laugh at the reaction of the small woman. She might have been elderly, but she didn't lack spunk and her tiny frame still stood straight underneath her hand-crocheted shawl.

"Please come in," Nana said as she ushered them into a living room. "At my age, I'll freeze to death just by looking at that storm out there. And it doesn't take much of a breeze to blow me away." Nana turned to Merri and smiled, waiting for something.

Merri opened her mouth to introduce herself, but Brighton jumped in first. "Since you didn't want to go into town to get your hair done in this storm, I brought someone up here to do it for you."

Nana's mouth dropped open again. "You didn't have to do that, Bright."

"I know, but I wanted to."

Merri stuck her hand out. "I'm Merri Wilcox. It's nice to meet you,"

Nana grasped Merri's hand with both of hers and hung on tightly. "*The* Merri Wilcox?" She raised her eyebrows and looked at Brighton.

"You've...heard of me?" Merri looked from Brighton to his grandmother through narrowed eyebrows. Bright red colored his cheeks, but she didn't know if the cause was embarrassment or the fact that they'd just walked two miles through a snowstorm. She suspected the latter.

"Are you the same Merri Wilcox that Bright went to school with?" Nana asked.

"Umm, yes. We went to school together."

Nana smiled but didn't say anything else.

Has my name come up in conversations between them before? She probably doesn't want me to cut her hair if she knows how much Brighton and I fought growing up.

"Were you able to make it down the lane without getting stuck?" Nana stepped to the front window and pulled the lacy curtains to one side so she could see out. "No one's been by to plow me out yet so I'm sure it wasn't easy."

Brighton looked at Merri. "Actually, we didn't even make it to your lane. I swerved to avoid hitting a deer and we slid into a drift...at the bottom of a slope."

Nana gasped and turned from the window. "That's horrible. Are you okay?"

"We're fine," Merri assured her. "Really."

"I think the car's fine, too. It's just really stuck. Neither of us could get a cell signal to call a tow truck so we decided to just keep walking. It was only a couple of miles."

Nana peered out her window again. "You walked a couple of miles in *this*?"

Merri smiled. "It only got bad the last little bit."

"Oh my goodness, come sit by the fire you poor

thing." Nana grabbed Merri's hand and dragged her to a chair in front of the fireplace. "You take those wet things off while I make you some hot cocoa."

"Thank you."

Merri unzipped her coat as Nana rushed off to the kitchen. Brighton sat down in a chair opposite her and began removing his own wet coat.

"She seems great," Merri said.

"Nana means a lot to me."

Merri laid her coat and gloves on the stone surrounding the fireplace and slipped out of her boots. Her socks were wet, too, but taking them off seemed to be going too far. She leaned forward, soaking in the warmth from the glowing fire.

To describe Nana's house as cozy would be an understatement. The arms of the couch had crocheted doilies on them, a pile of carefully folded handmade quilts sat in a basket between the couch and Brighton's chair, and a large Christmas tree—real, of course—sat in the corner of the room, decorated with gold and silver and red. It was everything she would imagine a mountain cabin to be.

Dozens of photographs lined the mantle above the fireplace. Adults and kids alike filled the photos, laughing, smiling, and posing. Merri searched the photos for Brighton but couldn't find any. Nana seemed to have a large family.

"You doing okay?" Brighton asked after they'd sat in silence for a few moments.

"I'm getting to that stage of thawing where everything starts to wake up and tingle. So yeah, I'll survive."

Brighton looked down at his hands. "I'm starting to see why you didn't like me much growing up."

Merri tilted her head and looked at him. "What do you mean?"

"I guilted you into coming with me today and now I've ruined your evening. When I want something, I go after it and I don't always think how it will affect other people. I wanted Nana to have a nice Christmas and I ruined your evening in the process. That wasn't my intention."

"It's not exactly ruined—just changed. My sister will get over it." Merri looked at her watch. "It's six. They're probably just sitting down to dinner, which is probably cheese pizza ordered in. It's kind of a holiday tradition. I should probably call and tell her I'm not going to be there."

Brighton immediately jumped up. "And I should probably call a tow truck. Maybe we can get out of here in time for you to make it to at least part of the evening." He hurried across the room and picked up a phone from its base. "You go first," he said as he handed the phone to her.

Merri pressed the button and put the phone to her ear, but heard nothing. "Are you sure this is plugged in?" she asked.

Brighton walked back to the phone base and jiggled the cords. "It's fine over here. Isn't it working?"

Merri shook her head just as Nana walked into the room with a steaming mug in each of her hands. "By the way, the phone lines have been out for hours. I figured you tried to call to tell me you weren't coming and couldn't get through. That's why I was so surprised when you showed up on my doorstep," Nana said.

Brighton pulled his cell from his pocket and looked at the screen. "Still no reception. Though I'm not surprised. I rarely have any up here."

"One more reason for me not to get one." Nana turned to Merri. "Bright keeps trying to convince me to get one of those cell thingies, but if I can't actually use it, what's the point?"

Merri laughed. "I think I'm on your side on this one."

"No way. There are areas up here where the phones work just fine. She's always going for walks. What if she falls and needs to call for help?" Brighton defended himself.

"You're making it sound like I'm an old woman," Nana said with a wink aimed at Merri.

With the cozy fire, the not-so-bad-as-she-thought company, and the soothing mug of hot cocoa tucked between her hands, Merri began to wonder if her evening would actually be better than one spent down home with Nicole's family.

"Nana, this is sooo good." Merri sighed contentedly as she took another bite of the homemade chicken noodle soup in front of her. Merri had offered to help make dinner, but Nana insisted she stay in the living room by the fire. After Brighton handed her a blanket, Merri curled up in an overstuffed recliner and unwillingly drifted off to sleep. She woke when Brighton tapped her shoulder, announcing dinner. Somehow, after only an hour of knowing she'd have company for dinner, Nana managed to set bowls of the best chicken noodle soup Merri had ever tasted on the table.

"When I was younger, I wanted to eat at Nana's house every night," Brighton said as he reached for another slice of homemade bread from a basket in the middle of the table. "This is just one of the reasons why."

"You two stop," Nana said. "You're going to make me blush."

"I only tell the truth," Brighton said. Merri noticed him check his cell phone again. He'd already done it twice just since they sat down to eat. With a frown, he stood and checked the house phone again. Nothing. "I'm starting to think we're not getting out of here tonight."

Nana looked up from her own bowl. "You are more than welcome to stay here if you can't get someone up here. You know you're always welcome here."

"I know. And thank you, but tomorrow is Christmas Eve and I'm sure Merri wants to be with her own family."

Nana nodded and smiled at Merri but didn't say anything.

Merri helped Nana clear the table while Brighton put his boots back on and announced that he would be shoveling the porch. When every dish had been washed, dried, and carefully placed back in Nana's cabinets, Merri stuck her head out the front door to talk to Brighton. "I hate to tell you this, but everywhere you cleared is already buried again."

Brighton turned and looked at the trail he'd shoveled. "Maybe so, but if I don't periodically clear the front door, and the storm continues, we'll literally be stuck inside the house until it all melts. That could take months."

Merri laughed. "By all means, shovel away then."

Twenty minutes later, Brighton came to the same conclusion that his efforts were indeed in vain and gave up, returning the shovel to its place next to the front door.

"Come inside and watch TV with us," Nana insisted. "I'll pop some popcorn."

Even though she shared the evening with two people she barely knew, Merri couldn't help but think that the evening spent by the fire with popcorn and blankets felt just like Christmas would with her family. Brighton flipped on the television and scanned the channels until a weather report came on.

"This storm is being called a Christmas miracle. No one suspected this weather system to produce so much snow, and in such a short amount of time. While the ski resorts are loving it, motorists in the valleys aren't finding as much joy." The camera panned to show the interstate, completely backed up with cars. *"People trying to finish last minute shopping or traveling to visit friends and family are advised to use caution. The roads are completely gridlocked at this time. Highway patrolmen have already received calls for 97 slide-offs and accidents today. James Harton, owner of Quicky Boys Towing said he's never been as busy as he has been today. Just as a reminder, the following roads are still closed: I-80 going through Parley's Canyon, Highway 189 between Park City and Heber City, and U-152 giving access to Big Cottonwood Canyon. Travel is being restricted to absolute emergencies. Stay tuned and we'll keep you updated on storm information and road conditions."*

Merri cleared her throat. "I guess that answers the question of where we'll be staying tonight."

Brighton frowned. "I'm so sorry, Merri."

"You keep saying that, but it's okay. Really. I'm not upset."

"We'll call a tow truck first thing in the morning and you'll be home for most of Christmas Eve."

"I always keep the guest room bed made up, but it rarely gets used. You can sleep there, Merri. The third bedroom is kind of my all purpose room and there's no bed in there so you'll have to sleep on the couch, Bright."

"I don't mind at all. Thanks, Nana."

Nana took Merri by the hand and led her to one of the three bedrooms in the hallway. "I'll show you around. We'll make sure the heat is turned on, too. I wouldn't want you to freeze all night."

Merri couldn't hold back her smile when she saw the interior of the room. A large, roughly hewn log bed took up much of the floor space. Next to the bed was a log nightstand with a lamp and a teddy bear clock. A patchwork quilt of every color and pattern covered the top of the bed. "Nana, did you make this?" Merri asked as she ran her hand along the top of the quilt. "It's beautiful."

Nana turned from the thermostat she'd been adjusting and looked at the quilt. "That old thing? I made it so many years ago, you probably weren't even alive."

"I think it's wonderful. I love anything that's colorful like this."

"I'm glad you like it. I want you to be comfortable while you're here."

A knock on the doorframe caused both women to turn. Brighton stood in the doorway, holding Merri's purse and the duffel bag full of hair cutting supplies. "I thought you might want these in here."

Merri took them from his hands and set them on the floor next to a rocking chair made in the same style as the bed. "Thanks."

"You'll have your own bathroom," Nana said, opening a door in the corner of the room and motioning inside. "There's just a shower, no tub. I hope that's okay."

"It's more than okay. I'm sure I'll have the best night's rest I've had in a long time."

"Well, now that we've decided you're definitely staying. I'm going to go to bed," Nana said. "You know me, Bright. I'm not a night owl."

Brighton stood with Nana and gave her a big hug. "Thanks for everything."

"Anytime, hon. Good night."

Merri glanced at the clock on the nightstand as Nana left. Eight thirty. If she went to bed right then, she'd be wide awake by four in the morning. She wondered how awkward it would be if she returned to the living room and watched TV with Brighton. Sure, he'd been nice enough that day, and she realized that neither of them was the same person they were in school, but they were still strangers. She didn't even know what he did for a living. Maybe he didn't work. Everyone knew his father had enough money to go around.

She'd finally decided to announce that she'd be going to bed too when Brighton spoke up. "Earlier today, you said you never beat me at anything."

She nodded slowly, not sure what he was leading up to.

"You were wrong."

Merri raised her eyebrows. "Care to clarify?"

58

"Mrs. Tubbs' class. Sixth grade."

"I'm still not following you."

"We were having a class party of some sort. I think we'd earned enough reading points to have a special day or something like that. Anyway, we got to play card games and board games in the afternoon. You and I played Uno with a couple other kids and you won."

A smile slowly spread across Merri's face. "I can't believe I forgot about that. You'd think my one moment of triumph would be burned into my permanent memory."

"You reminded me about it for the first few months. The next time we got a chance in class, we had a rematch. I won that time."

"Of course you did. No wonder I pushed the memory from my brain."

Brighton grinned. "What do you say? Best out of three?"

Chapter 7

&

"Do you just happen to have Uno cards with you?" Merri asked. "I'm sorry to tell you this, but I don't make a habit of carrying a deck around with me."

"I don't have any, but Nana has every classic game you can think of, if you can find it," Brighton answered.

"Lead the way." Merri followed Brighton out of the guest room to a small laundry room just off the kitchen. A closet in the room revealed floor-to-ceiling shelving. The shelves were so laden with games that some of them drooped under the weight. "Wow. You weren't kidding. She really does have every game imaginable."

"I'd never joke about something as serious as an Uno battle." Brighton winked.

Merri felt herself starting to blush and turned away. "Just wait until I beat you again. You might not be as candid." Together they searched the closet for the familiar game. Five minutes later, Merri saw the cards tucked against the side of one shelf. "Found it!"

"Good. 'Cause it is on, baby."

Merri raised her eyebrows. "Baby?" She never expected *that* word to come from *that* mouth when referring to her.

"Sorry," Brighton stammered. "Would you prefer Your Highness?"

"No. I want you to call me The Champion."

Merri and Brighton took the deck of Uno cards to the kitchen table and Brighton shuffled them. He tried to do one of the fancy shuffling tricks she'd only seen at magic shows, but his attempts fell short.

"Are you trying to show off?" Merri asked as she crouched to pick up the dozen cards that tumbled to the floor. "If you are, it's not working."

Brighton concentrated on the deck in his hand. "My older brother and sister always made this look so easy. Every time I tried, they laughed at me."

"So you're saying I should stop laughing at you?"

Brighton looked at her with his half-grin. "Your laughter is cute. Theirs was mocking and usually accompanied by something along the lines of 'Give it up, little brother, you're never going to be as good as us so you might as well not try.'"

Merri frowned. Despite his smile, she sensed his story caused more pain than he let on. "I don't remember you having siblings. How many?"

Brighton nodded and then, giving up on the shuffling trick, began to deal the cards. "Just the two. They're both quite a bit older than me. They were already in high school when we moved to Salt Lake City."

61

"Do you see them a lot now that *you're* older?"

Brighton looked at her and shrugged. "Yeah. We see each other." He picked up his cards and carefully looked at each one as he splayed them in his hand. "I dealt so you go first."

She sensed he didn't want to talk about his family anymore so she dropped the subject and threw down a red three on top of the green three displayed.

"Changing it up already, I see," Brighton muttered. "That's fine. I've still got this." He tossed a green six onto the pile.

"Hmm...I'm out of green. I guess I'll just have to change the color." Merri added a Draw Four to the stack of cards on the table.

"Seriously? Already?" Brighton drew the cards, but the damage couldn't be repaired and Merri easily won the game.

"The Champion is back!" she yelled. Then, remembering that Nana slept just down the hall, she covered her mouth and whispered, "Oops. Sorry."

Brighton stacked the cards into one pile and handed them to Merri. "What do you say? Best out of five?"

"You're on."

They played two more games, each winning one, so Merri still stood as champion.

"Best out of seven?" Brighton asked after she tossed the last card in her hand onto the pile.

"Uh uh. No way. You'll just keep playing until you're back on top."

"True." He sighed. "I concede. You win."

"You gave in way easier than I expected. The Brighton Stansbury I know would never have conceded after one battle."

"What are you proposing?"

Merri nodded toward the laundry room. "There's an entire closet full of games in there."

A slow smile spread across Brighton's face. "You're on. Up next, a game of Sorry."

They pulled the game from the cupboard and set it up on the kitchen table. "I'll be red and you be green. After all, it's Christmastime."

They fought a hard battle, but Brighton won in the end. He stretched and pretended to yawn. "I'm back on top. I guess we can go to bed now."

Merri looked at her watch. "It's only nine-thirty, lightweight. Or maybe I should call you chicken." *I can't believe I'm still flirting with him. What is wrong with me!*

"Fine. Your turn to pick a game."

"Hmm…I choose Scrabble."

Brighton groaned. "Really?"

"Really. I'm good at that one."

They set the game up and fished through the overturned tiles as they prepared for the first round. Merri cleared her throat. "I should probably know this, and maybe you already told me, but what do you do? For a job, I mean."

Brighton looked down and frowned a little. Merri didn't know if the frown came in response to the question or his concentration on the tiles in front of him. "I work for the Stansbury Corporation."

"So you work with your dad?"

Brighton nodded. Still looking at his tiles.

"That's probably fun, being with him every day. I can't imagine my dad cutting hair next to me."

Brighton shrugged. "It pays the bills."

Merri thought of the sports car Brighton drove the

first day he came to *The Cut* and the SUV sitting in a snow drift a couple of miles away. She looked at his expensive jeans and designer label shirt. His job did a lot more than pay the bills. He'd been a clothes snob when they were younger. It didn't look like things had changed much.

Brighton obviously didn't want to go into detail, but Merri couldn't let the subject drop. He already knew more about her than she cared to admit. "Do your brother and sister work for your dad, too?"

He nodded. "And so does my sister's husband."

"Keeping it all in the family. I like that."

Another shrug.

"What about your mom? Does she work, too?"

Brighton finally looked up and shook his head. "Dad always liked her staying home. To take care of us and be a good housewife."

"I'm sure it was nice having her around all the time."

A hint of a smile played on his lips. "She managed to fill her time."

The game of Scrabble lasted for forty minutes. Although she eventually won, Merri had to fight for some of the words she wanted to use that Brighton questioned. Since neither of their cell phones worked, and the home didn't have internet access, they had to search Nana's bookcases until they found a dictionary so she could prove that her words were indeed real.

"If my count is correct, I'm the Uno champ and the Scrabble champ. You've only won Sorry. I guess that means I'm ahead."

Brighton crossed his arms over his chest. "I'm not done yet. We'll stay up all night if we have to. I'm getting Battleship."

And that's how the evening continued. Brighton won a well-fought game of Battleship, but Merri came back and won a game of Old Maid. Brighton won Candyland, but Merri won Connect 4.

"I can't believe the collection of games Nana has," Merri said as she unpacked Chutes and Ladders onto the table. A quick glance at her watch showed that it was past eleven.

"She used to play a lot of them with me when I was younger. If she were still awake she'd probably still be playing them with us."

"You're really close to here, aren't you? My grandparents all died when I was kind of young. I didn't get to know any of them in my adult years."

Brighton opened his mouth to say something, but then stopped. He looked toward the hall with Nana's room and then simply said, "Yes. We're close."

By the time Brighton won Chutes and Ladders, Merri could barely hold back her yawns. "Okay. We're even now. Maybe we should just leave it at that."

Brighton stuck his hand out. "I like that idea. We'll call it a truce. It will be like the Christmas truce during World War I. We better shake on it." He stuck his hand out and Merri took it, shaking it firmly. She started to pull her hand away, but Brighton continued to hold it. "Good night, Merri. Thanks for coming with me today."

She felt her cheeks warm and turn red as she suddenly became overly aware of his fingers wrapped around hers. Shaking herself, she pulled her hand away. "Good night, Brighton."

Alone in the guest room, Merri struggled to fall asleep even though she was physically and emotionally tired. Her mind replayed the events of the day and the times she and Brighton interacted in their youth, trying to balance the man he'd become with the boy he used to be. They didn't seem to be the same person at all. *Did he change or have I always been wrong about him? Or is he still the same obnoxious boy, but I want him to be different so I overlook the faults?*

She didn't know the answers to her questions, but she did know one thing. Her hand still tingled from Brighton's touch.

Merri's eyes fluttered open and she snuggled farther under the thick patchwork quilt covering her. The only part of her body not covered by the blankets or the soft pillow was her nose. She could faintly smell the fire burning in the wood stove out in the living room. Waking up like that every morning would be heaven. Her eyes slowly closed again.

Tap. Tap. Tap.

Merri's eyes popped open that time. No wonder she'd woken up the first time. Someone was knocking on her door.

She cleared her throat. "Yes?"

"Hey, Merri. It's Brighton. Nana wanted me to let you know that breakfast will be ready in half an hour."

"Okay. Thanks!" she called.

Half an hour. That meant she could stay in the comfort of the bed for at least five more minutes before she absolutely had to get up and take a shower. Her eyes flicked to the clock on the bedside table. 8:43 a.m. She gasped and sat up. She never slept that long. Nana's bed had been way too comfortable.

Merri swung her legs over the side of the bed and pulled the ties of the bathrobe Nana lent her to sleep in tighter around her waist. She'd give anything for clean clothes, or at least her toothbrush. She shuffled to the bathroom and reached behind the shower curtain to turn the water on. She let the warm water flow over her body for far longer than she should before reluctantly switching the lever to off. She wrapped herself in a fluffy white towel and returned to the bedroom where she dressed in the same clothes she'd worn the day before. "Thank heavens I'm a stylist," she whispered to herself as she dug through the bag of hair supplies she'd brought with her. Between the products in her bag and the spare makeup she always kept in her purse, she managed to make herself look normal despite the reused clothing.

She opened her bedroom door and stepped out into the hall just as Brighton emerged from the main bathroom. His hair looked freshly washed and he ran his fingers through it, giving it a messy look, but in a flattering way. A day's worth of stubble covered his chin and cheeks, making him appear more rugged than usual. She forced herself to look away. "Morning."

"Good morning. Did you sleep alright?"

"I don't think I've ever slept that good in my life."

"I'm glad."

"How about you?"

"As good as you can sleep on a couch."

"Sorry."

"It wasn't bad."

Merri's stomach growled when she smelled the aromas coming from the kitchen. She hoped Brighton didn't hear it.

"Nana, you didn't need to do all of this," Brighton said as they entered the room together.

"Yes I did. It's tradition. Even if you weren't here, I'd cook my famous Christmas Eve breakfast."

Merri closed her eyes and inhaled deeply. "It smells wonderful."

"My mother used to make flapjacks like these when I was a young girl. I carried on the tradition with my own family. There's a secret ingredient."

"You better let me have the recipe so I can continue the tradition," Brighton said.

"As soon as you get married, I'll give the recipe to you as a wedding gift."

"Sounds like a fair deal."

"Are you sure about that?" Nana asked. "You figuring out the secret ingredient might be easier than finding a girl willing to put up with you."

Merri giggled and Nana winked at her. Brighton glared at both of them.

The table held hash browns, scrambled eggs, and bacon. Merri thought for sure the table would collapse by the time Nana added a platter of steaming pancakes to the mix.

"One bite and you'll be hooked," Brighton said.

"I don't doubt that," Merri said as she added two pancakes to her already overflowing plate. "Just the smell has me hooked."

Brighton handed her a warm container of creamy syrup that smelled like cinnamon. "The homemade syrup makes it even better."

"Homemade syrup? Seriously?" She took the container and drizzled it all over her plate. "Mmm... These are unbelievable. I have to be dreaming." She sighed and closed her eyes as she chewed.

"See, Nana. I told you they were the best," Brighton said.

"I already knew that." Nana smiled as she tossed another pancake onto Merri's plate. "Have you guessed the secret ingredient?"

Merri tilted her head. "There's definitely cinnamon in there. And nutmeg, I think. And there's something else. Something...like...I can't quite put my finger on it."

Nana nodded. "That's the same problem everyone has when they try them for the first time."

"I could eat these every day. *Everything* on the plate is wonderful."

After sufficiently stuffing themselves, Merri volunteered to clear the table while Brighton went to shovel the front porch and walk again. Somehow doing housework in Nana's house felt different than it did in her own apartment—fun even. She enjoyed the coziness and warmth of the home and felt sad that she no longer had living grandparents to visit. *I wonder if Brighton will invite me to cut Nana's hair again...*

Shaking herself from her thoughts, Nana turned to the elderly woman working on a puzzle in a crossword book. "Are you ready for me to do you hair, Nana?" she asked. "We never did get around to it last night. After all that's happened, I better at least do what I came here for."

The elderly woman laughed. "Well by all means, let's do it. Brighton tells me you have a reputation for being the best in the valley."

"I don't know about that. I just opened my own salon a few months ago. It's been a huge process but I'm having fun."

"I'm sure you'll be great. At my age, there's not a

lot to work with, which means there's not a lot to mess up." Nana set her pen on the table and closed the crossword book. "After all the trouble Brighton and I have put you through the last couple of days, I'm going to owe you a lot for this haircut."

Merri smiled. "Except for the whole burying-the-car-in-a-snowdrift-and-having-to-hike-through-a-storm thing, the experience hasn't been too bad. This haircut is on me."

"We'll see."

Chapter 8

✂

Merri shook her head and returned to the guest room for the bag full of supplies. As she walked past the living room window on her return to the kitchen, she caught a glimpse of Brighton shoveling the front walk. She stepped to the window and lifted the sheer curtains just enough to look out. The snow had finally stopped, but it left chaos in its wake. At that point, Brighton had made very little progress on the mounds of snow, but didn't seem to be giving up. As Merri watched, he took off his glove and wiped a hand across his glistening forehead. For some reason, watching him like that, hard at work, Merri's heart started beating just a little faster. Brighton started to turn his head toward the window. Not wanting him to catch her spying, she quickly dropped the curtain and continued into the kitchen.

Merri spread her supplies on the table and chose a chair for Nana to sit in while she worked. She wrapped a black cape around Nana's shoulders and a smock around her own.

"Do you mind if I drop the clippings on the floor or would you rather I put a tarp down?" Merri asked. She didn't have a tarp and hoped Nana didn't mind her kitchen floor being temporarily treated like the floor of *The Cut*.

"These floors have seen far worse. Go ahead and cut. I can sweep and mop later."

Merri worked in silence for the first few minutes, but then Nana cleared her throat.

"I can't believe after all these years I finally got to meet you," Nana said. "I didn't think it would ever happen."

Merry stopped cutting. "What do you mean? You know who I am?"

"Brighton used to tell me everything about school. He's quite a talker as you probably know."

Actually, I don't know. Surprisingly, we've never talked that much. He kept his personal life out of our feud.

"Your name came up many times over the years he was in school."

Merri sighed. "I hope you don't believe everything he said. Remember there are always two sides to a story."

Nana laughed at that. "Don't worry. I only heard good things. I have to admit, though, after he graduated without getting the guts to actually ask you out, I thought his chance had passed. I didn't know you were in his life again," Nana said. "How long have the two of you been dating?"

Merri swallowed hard and shook her head quickly even though Nana couldn't see her face. "Oh no. I think you've gotten the wrong impression. We're not dating. At all. We've never dated actually. Apparently Brighton heard about my new salon and came in. He didn't know I owned it until I told him. I guess since he knew me from our school days, he figured it would be safe to ask me if I'd come up here with him to cut your hair. There's no relationship." The words rushed out and by the time she finished, Merri wasn't sure if any of the things she'd just blurted made any sense.

Nana chuckled a little. "Maybe you should put the boy out of his misery and ask him out yourself."

Huh? Sorry Nana, but you have a greater chance of pigs learning how to fly. "Put him out of his misery?"

"Sure."

Nana didn't elaborate and Merri didn't dare question her further. The conversation wasn't going as planned. Rather than continue the awkwardness and the twisting of her stomach, Merri decided to change the topic before it got completely out of hand. "So, Nana, is Brighton's father your son or is his mother your daughter? I don't think he mentioned it to me. And I'm sorry to admit it, but I don't know your actual name."

Nana laughed and Merri had to stop cutting while her little body shook with the motion. "Actually, I'm neither. As far as I know, there is no familial relationship between me and Brighton."

"But...I thought...he calls you..." Merri was at a loss for words.

"When Bright's family moved to Utah, my husband and I lived next door to their home in the valley. I watched him grow from boy to man so I guess I feel like he's family. I've never met a more polite boy. He used to volunteer to mow my lawn in the summer and shovel my snow in the winter. As a boy, he'd pick up my newspaper from the driveway on his way to school every morning and leave it on our doorstep. I never paid him a cent to do any of that stuff. What teenage boy does that?"

Merri took her time answering. If Brighton Stansbury could be that sweet to his elderly neighbor, why had he spent the same years torturing her? "None that I've ever known about," Merri finally said. "Are you sure we're talking about the same person?"

Nana continued her praise. "He never missed a week of calling me during the years he was away at college and his kindnesses have continued on into adulthood."

"I had no idea."

"My husband passed during Brighton's senior year of high school. I think that cemented him into my life. He became my right hand man. As you've probably noticed from the pictures on the mantle, I have three children of my own. All three were out of the house before the Stansbury family moved to the neighborhood. And sadly, all three now live too far away to visit without the use of an airplane and a layover or two. I don't get to see them or my grandkids very often these days."

At least that explains why Brighton isn't in her family pictures. "I'm sorry. That must be hard."

"It is. They stay in touch, of course. But it's not the same as having my grandkids physically present to smother with hugs."

"Do you still have a home by the Stansbury family in the valley?"

"Oh no. I sold it four years ago. It was too much for me to keep up with and I no longer had the desire. I decided to sell it to another family who was ready to make memories of their own. This place," Nana motioned to the walls around her, "was built by my father almost a hundred years ago. My husband and I always tried to keep it in top condition. When the opportunity to sell my valley home came up, I knew there was only one place I cared to go permanently."

"It must be hard being so secluded, especially in the winter."

"That is true, but Brighton watches out for me. If he didn't, I'd hire people to shovel snow and bring me groceries. I might be old, but I know how to take care of myself."

Merri smiled. "You're not old, you're just wise."

Nana chuckled. "He really did talk about you all the time, you know."

"Excuse me?" Merri felt herself blush as she snipped at Nana's thin, white hair. *I guess we're back to that conversation.*

"Oh yes. He talked about you more than anyone else. He might not have been willing to admit it back then, but he definitely had a crush on you."

Merri's blush deepened and she was grateful that there wasn't a mirror in the kitchen like in *The Cut.*

"He felt horrible for months after running against you for student body president. He moped about it for so long, his father finally sent him off on some long excursion in Europe."

"Why would he be upset? Brighton *won* that election."

"Oh, I know that," Nana said quickly. "But when Bright found out you were running, too, he decided to run for vice president instead. His father found out and threw a fit. He wouldn't let him change his intended office. No son of his would run for second place, he insisted." Nana took a deep breath before mumbling, "I declare, that man is insufferable."

This was the first time Merri had heard any of this. "Why would Brighton want to change just because I was running against him? Was he actually worried that he'd lose to me?" Merri stepped in front of Nana to test the length of the hair resting on the woman's forehead. "Once I heard *he* would be running, I knew *I* didn't stand a chance of winning."

"He wasn't worried that he'd lose. He was worried that he'd win. He didn't want to do that to you."

Merri felt tears spring to her eyes at the realization that Brighton had been willing to give up his candidacy for her sake. Not wanting Nana to see, she quickly stepped behind the chair again. Had all those years of teasing and pranks really been flirting like her friends sometimes suggested? She'd built a wall against Brighton so high, she didn't know how to knock it down.

Nana sighed. "I thought the poor boy was through with his father, but he keeps coming back to haunt him."

Merri pulled the cape from Nana's shoulders and shook the hair onto the floor. "Did Mr. Stansbury pass away? I hadn't heard that."

Nana laughed. "Heaven's no. We could never be that lucky. Didn't Bright tell you about their falling out?"

"I was being honest when I said I hadn't spoken to him since our senior year. I went to the University of Utah and Brighton left for...wherever it was he went to school."

"I guess you wouldn't know then, would you?

Bright's father insisted he go to Harvard."

"He definitely had the grades for it."

"True, but he didn't want to go there."

"Why not?"

"Bright's father wanted him to study business, which they both agreed on, but his father wanted him to study at Harvard because that's where he went and it would look impressive when he joined the family business. Bright wanted to study at the University of Pennsylvania because they were ranked so high in finance and management and he liked their philanthropy courses. His goal was to start his own business, completely separate from his father's, that managed charities and non-profits. It might not be Harvard, but it's still an impressive Ivy League school."

"Where did he end up going?"

Nana smiled. "He stuck to his guns and went to the University of Pennsylvania."

"I'm guessing Mr. Stansbury wasn't very happy about that decision."

"That's the understatement of the year."

"What happened?"

"His father cut him off. The endless money supply ended and Bright had to pay for all his schooling himself. Sure, he got a few scholarships and that helped, but as I'm sure you know, the cost of tuition, and books, and room and board is insanely expensive."

Merri groaned. "I know that all too well."

"Maybe it's not my business to tell you, but even though he worked while he went to school, and tried for the first time in his life to understand what it means to be frugal, he still amassed quite a few student loans."

"I'll be paying mine off for a while still."

Nana turned to Merri with sadness in her eyes. "Bright opened his dream company after he graduated and put his heart and soul into it, but he just couldn't make enough to pay off his debts and still keep the company afloat."

Merri thought of the multiple cars Brighton still drove. Apparently the lessons in frugality weren't sticking. "I thought he told me he worked with his dad."

"He does. After he realized his business wouldn't make it unless he could get more backing, he had to come crawling back to his father. His father signed a contract with him that he'd give him the startup cash he needed as long as he agreed to work with the Stansbury Corporation for ten years."

"Ten years?" Merri gasped.

Nana nodded. "Poor guy. He didn't have any other choice. He's been miserable. All his dreams have been crushed."

Merri felt like her heart would break as she thought of the mean things she'd said to Brighton on the drive through the canyon the day before. The tears finally spilled onto her cheeks as she whispered, "Why didn't he tell me?"

"What was that dear?" Nana asked.

Before Merri could respond, Brighton stepped into the kitchen. "I just checked and the phone lines are working again. I tried to get a tow truck, but apparently the roads are still closed. I'm so sorry I did this to you on Christmas Eve, Merri." He took a step toward her and she quickly bent down to refill her bag of supplies. If she looked him in the eyes, he might see the tears of guilt that remained there. "I wasn't planning on opening *The Cut* today anyway. And my Christmas shopping is done. I'm sure we'll be out of here by this afternoon. No big deal."

Nana stood from the chair and clapped her hands together. "Good! I'm glad I get the two of you for a while longer. I need someone to help me eat all the goodies I've been stockpiling up here. Some of the people spending holidays in their cabins have been bringing things by. And I still haven't made my molasses cookies. Do you like molasses cookies, Merri?"

Merri brushed a hand across her face, removing the remaining remnants of tears. "I love them."

"Good. Give me one minute to freshen up and I'll get started on them."

Merri reached for the broom next to the refrigerator to sweep up the hair as Nana left the room, but Brighton took it from her and began to brush it across the floor. He didn't say anything to her, but she suddenly felt extremely awkward being alone with him. If all the things Nana said were true, Brighton wasn't anything like the person she'd always thought he was. She tried to look at him with new eyes. *If I'd never met him, and didn't go to school with him, and only knew the things Nana just told me, I would think Brighton Stansbury was the world's greatest catch. So...is he?*

He turned to her then and gave her his famous half-smile. "Is there something you'd like to say? I can feel you staring at me."

Merri looked away, embarrassed. "I was just wondering if you got the snow all cleared from the front."

"Not even close. That's some heavy snow out there. I'm headed back out in a minute. I thought I'd take a break to check on you and Nana."

"Check on us? You don't trust us?" Merri smiled.

Brighton emptied the dustpan of white hair into the trash and returned the broom to its spot behind the fridge. "I trust you. It's Nana I'm not sure about. There's no filter on that mouth when it comes to keeping secrets."

"Ooo...what kind of secrets is she keeping?"

"I'm afraid she might give away the location of my secret lair."

"I'd never give that away," Nana said, entering the kitchen again. "Some things are just too important."

Merri laughed. "Do you need help with the cookies, Nana?"

"You've already done the dishes and my hair this morning and you're my guest. I'll let you help me eat them when they're done."

"Deal."

Brighton zipped up his coat and pulled his gloves on again. "I'm headed back out. The snow thinks it can conquer me, but I intend to show it who's boss."

"I'm going to call Nicole. She's probably wondering what happened to me last night," Merri said. She waited until Brighton closed the front door to make the call. "Nicole? It's me," she said when her sister picked up.

"*Where have you been? Your phone kept going to voicemail and you never showed up last night. I thought you'd been abducted.*"

"You thought I'd been abducted?"

"*Sure. An attractive woman living alone is the perfect target for creeps. Seriously though, where are you? I called Paige last night and she told me you left with one of the hot Stansbury guys to cut his grandmother's hair. I assumed she meant Brighton since you told me he'd been in contact with you."*

"You're right. He convinced me to come up the canyon with him to cut her hair so she wouldn't have to go out in the weather."

"But all the roads were closed last night."

"Exactly. That's why we couldn't leave. The phone lines were down and I couldn't get any cell reception up here." She didn't bother telling Nicole about sliding off the road and burying their vehicle in the snow.

"Are you going to be home tonight? You have to be here for Christmas Eve."

"I'll try. The roads are still closed, though." *And then we'll have to get a tow truck...*

"Okay. Be safe. And have fun with Brighton."

Merri sensed amusement in Nicole's voice. "I'll call you as soon as I get home."

Merri hung up the phone and looked around the room. Nana had kicked her out of the kitchen and Brighton had returned to his endless shoveling. Having no desire to just sit around with her thoughts, she walked to the fireplace where her coat, gloves, and boots still sat and put them on.

"Need some help?" she called as she poked her head through the front door.

Brighton turned at the sound of her voice. "Sure. Then maybe you'll believe me when I tell you how heavy it is."

"Or, I'll easily clear the snow and make you look like...well, a wimp."

"It will never happen."

True, Merri thought as she considered his toned

abs and arms. *And especially not after the things Nana just told me.*

Chapter 9

✂

The cold air hit instantly when Merri stepped onto the front porch and she sucked in her breath sharply. All of the front steps and about eight feet of the front walk were completely cleared. That just left the other thirty feet of the walk and the half-mile of driveway.

"Wow. This is deep," she said.

"I know. I measured and it's almost two and a half feet. Not bad for a twenty-four hour period."

"No kidding. I wonder how much they got in the valley?"

"Nana had the news turned on before you woke up this morning and they were reporting almost two feet."

"I can't remember the last time we had a storm this big."

"I can. It was our senior year."

Merri raised her eyebrows at him. "You seem pretty sure of that answer."

"I remember because it came right after Nana's husband died. We could hardly walk through the deep snow at the cemetery when they buried him."

Merri thrust her shovel into the ground and lifted. Brighton hadn't exaggerated the heaviness of the snow and she struggled to lift the fully loaded shovel, but she wasn't about to admit that to him. Instead, she cleared her throat and asked, "Why did you make me think Nana is your grandmother?"

Brighton threw a shovelful of snow to his side, keeping his head down. "I never said she was my grandma."

"Maybe not, but you must have known I thought that."

"I guess I think of her as a grandma. Does it matter?"

Merri thought about it. "No. Not really. But I think you used the poor old grandma card to convince me to come up here with you in the first place."

"She *is* old."

"Yeah, but she would have survived without a haircut until after the storm passed."

"How many times do I have to say I'm sorry?"

"I'm not mad. I like Nana," Merri said quickly. "My grandparents have all passed away. I wish I still had one to make me cookies on a regular basis."

"We can share her. Every time she needs a haircut I can bring you back up here."

"Thanks, but maybe you better bring her to me. I've seen how you drive."

"A deer running out into the middle of the road could have happened to anyone. The fact that I avoided hitting it should say something about my driving skills."

"I've never driven off the side of the road while trying to avoid a deer," Merri teased.

"The roads were slippery."

"I feel like you're looking for excuses," she continued to tease.

"You're welcome to drive on the way home."

"If we ever make it home. Considering how dense this snow is, it might take four tow trucks to pull you out."

Brighton smiled sheepishly. "Come on, it wasn't buried that bad."

"Maybe not at the time, but by now you might not find it until spring."

"Sadly, there's some truth to that statement."

The two continued working side by side at a snail's pace. Merri's arms shook beneath her coat from lifting heavy shovelful after heavy shovelful, but she didn't want to be the first to quit. Lost in her thoughts, Merri didn't notice that Brighton had stopped working next to her—until a snowball hit her in the back of the head.

Shocked, she whipped around to glare at Brighton who already had another snowball formed and aimed at her. "You did *not* just do that."

"I did. And I don't regret it." He grinned. "Although, admittedly, I was aiming for your back, not your head."

"So not only can you not drive straight, but you can't throw straight either," Merri said.

Without any further warning, Brighton pulled his arm back and unleashed the second snowball. It connected with her face, splattering across her cheeks and dripping down into her coat. "Hey, look at that. My aim's not so bad after all," he said.

"You're going to regret doing that." Still gasping from the cold shock, Merri grabbed a handful of snow and hurled it at Brighton. He easily ducked and the poorly formed ball sailed over his head.

"Is that the best you've got?"

"You are so frustrating!" Merri yelled.

"No I'm not. You just think I am because you're frustrated with yourself."

Merri grabbed another handful of snow, taking her time as she formed it into a perfectly packed ball. She raised her arm and thrust it forward, faking a throw. Brighton dodged the empty pass, just as she knew he would. While he struggled to regain his balance, she unleashed the snowball for real, hitting him square in the chest.

"That was a dirty trick," Brighton said as he brushed the snow from his coat. He bent to gather another handful of snow and Merri took that as her cue to leave. The snow was deep and came past her knees so she only made it a foot or two before Brighton nailed her in the back. She didn't turn around, but continued her struggle through the snow until she reached the safety of one of the big pine trees. Peeking around from the green branches, she saw Brighton kneeling on the section of front walk they'd already cleared of snow, making a pile of snowballs.

"What is this? Grade school?" Merri called.

"What are you saying?" Brighton called back.

"Aren't we a little old for this?"

"Come on, Merri. No one's ever too old for a snowball fight."

Brighton's camp was directly between her position and the safety the front door promised. Realizing there was no way out of her predicament, Merri bent and began making her own pile. At least there wouldn't be a shortage of snow around her territory.

"Are you ready yet?" Brighton called a few minutes later.

"Uhh…" Merri looked at her pile of snowballs and compared it to Brighton's. His larger hands had been able to work faster, but she had shelter from the tree. Brighton must have interpreted her hesitation as readiness because before she could say anything else, he unleashed a volley of snowballs.

Merri screamed and dove behind the tree, knocking snow off the pine needles and down the back of her coat as she did so. Shivering, she jumped back up when the sound of thumping snowballs died off and sent her own volley across the yard. "You missed me!" she yelled, not even looking up as she hurled each snowball. When Brighton didn't answer, she stopped her barrage and looked in his direction. Instead of strands of dark hair poking out from his stocking cap, she saw nothing. Brighton had vanished.

"Brighton?"

Nothing.

"Did you surrender already? I knew you were a chick—"

Before she could finish her sentence, a figure darted from around the other side of her tree and tackled her to the ground. She screamed, terrified, until she opened her eyes and saw Brighton's laughing eyes looking back at her.

"What was that you were going to say?" he said.

Merri lay on her back, Brighton pinning her arms out on either side of her body. She tried to act mad, but couldn't suppress an escaping giggle. "Nothing. I wasn't going to say anything."

"You know what I think?" Brighton grinned.

Merri shook her head.

"I think you're in the perfect position for a face full of snow."

Merri gasped. "You wouldn't dare."

Brighton let go of one of her hands to grab some snow, but she used her freedom to her advantage and slugged him in the stomach with her gloved hand.

Brighton groaned and fell into the snow next to her. "That was low," he grunted, but a smile played on his lips.

Merri rolled over to face him. "Truce?" she said, sticking her hand out.

"Truce." He shook her hand.

In that position, their faces were only inches from each other. Merri's stomach twisted itself in knots. She quickly sat up and Brighton did the same thing, avoiding further eye contact.

"I guess we should get back to shoveling," she said.

"You're probably right," Brighton agreed, but neither of them made an effort to move.

The silence between them grew. Merri knew she couldn't live with the unanswered questions she had about Brighton. Taking a deep breath, she plunged forward. "Why didn't you tell me you tried to run for vice president instead of president our senior year?"

Brighton stared at the ground. "I shouldn't have left you alone with Nana."

"Why didn't you want me to know?" she asked quietly.

Brighton shrugged and absent-mindedly picked at the pine needles on the tree. "It's complicated."

"Because of your dad?"

"Nana didn't hold anything back, did she."

Merri looked down at her gloved hands. "It's nice that you tried to help me out, even though I didn't know about it."

"When my dad wouldn't cave about me running for vice president, I thought maybe you could run for that instead. We could have worked together. Personally, I thought we'd make a good team."

Merri thought back to the high school election. She had a vague memory of Brighton approaching her in the hall and suggesting that exact scenario. "When you brought it up all those years ago, I thought you were just trying to put me down. You know, tell me I'd never win and I should give up without trying."

Brighton started shaking his head before Merri finished her sentence. "No way. I didn't dare stand up to my dad back then and he was forcing me to run for president. I thought I might win and I didn't want to do that to you. I knew you cared about it more than I did. It was a close race."

Merri laughed. "No it wasn't. I saw the results. You won by a landslide. And as much as I don't want to admit it, you did a good job. Our senior year was awesome."

"It was fun, wasn't it?"

"If you thought I'd do a good job, why were you so mean to me all the time?"

Brighton shook his head. "Are we still talking about this? People change, Merri."

"Do they?"

Brighton gave Merri a long look. "Maybe not

89

everyone. You still can't let go of high school. I've never met anyone as stubborn as you."

"Me? *Stubborn?*"

"Yes."

"Let's talk about you for a minute. You had everything. Friends, money, the attention of every girl in every grade...I mean, I don't think there was a single girl you didn't date back then. Why did you have to harass me all the time?"

"I could pose the same question to you."

"I only responded to *your* harassment. You were the one that egged everything on. Always. And by the way, I never had the money to buy friends like you did. I had to come about them the normal way. You know, by being nice and supporting them."

Brighton's nostrils flared. "You know nothing about me."

Merri jumped up. "Nana tried to paint a different picture of you just now, but all I know is what I witnessed for years."

"I guess I was wrong about you. I thought you were different. I thought you weren't as shallow as every other person I've ever met."

Merri clenched her hands into fists. "Let me know when the tow truck gets here...if you can handle that much effort in my behalf." She turned and stomped through the snow, fighting back the tears that threatened to fall. She refused to give Brighton the satisfaction of seeing her cry.

"Back so soon? It must be cold out there," Nana's shaky voice greeted her as soon as she entered the home. "I almost have the first batch of cookies done."

"Thank you, Nana. If you don't mind, I think I'll lay down for a bit."

"By all means. I always take an afternoon nap myself."

Merri grabbed a book off the bookshelf in the corner as she passed through the room. She didn't bother looking at the title. All she needed was something to distract her from her thoughts. As she sat in the rocking chair in the guest room and pulled a crocheted afghan around her shoulders, she finally looked at the title—*Backyard Delight: Attracting Native Birds.*

"Lovely," Merri muttered as she tossed the book onto the comforter of the bed. She rocked back and forth, trying to relieve some of the anger building up inside. *Am I stubborn and shallow? In high school, Brighton drove a brand new car, he never wore the same thing twice, and he dated a different girl every week. In high school, he laughed at everything I did—be it bad or good. In high school, he— Crap. He's right. I can't let go of high school. I need to apologize.*

But I hate apologizing.

Come on, Merri. You're an adult. You can do this.

She stood and took a deep breath before marching toward the bedroom door and opening it. She jumped back in surprise when she saw Brighton standing there, his arm raised as if he were about to knock.

"I come bearing gifts," he said, thrusting a plate of warm molasses cookies toward her.

"Thanks." Merri took them from his hand and inhaled the sweet aroma. Intoxicating.

"Merri, I need to apol—"

"Brighton, I need to apol—"

They both spoke at the same time and then stopped, smiling. "Ladies first," Brighton said.

Merri stepped back into the room and sat on the

bed. Brighton followed her and sat in the rocking chair. "You were right. I can't let go of high school. I'm not sure why. I feel like every time I turned around you were there, involved in everything bad that happened to me. It's not fair to you to keep judging you by those days. I'm sorry."

"Apology accepted. And I apologize to you, too. I know I took some of the pranks and harassment too far back then. I know we didn't act like it, but I thought of you as my one honest friend."

Merri raised her eyebrows in surprise.

"Do you know why everyone wanted to hang out with me back then? It's not hard to guess and you've already pointed it out. Everybody wanted to hang out with me because they thought they'd get something for nothing. I never knew who liked me for me and who liked me for monetary reasons. That's why I dated so many girls. I never trusted any of their motives so I bounced from girl to girl. You were the only one, male or female, that didn't throw yourself at me. You were the only one that didn't care about my status or how your status would change if you were seen talking to me in the hall. I think I was afraid if I let you get too close to me I'd end up losing the one person I could trust so I pushed you away. I'm sorry."

Merri nodded. "Apology accepted."

"Can we start over? You know, pretend we've never met?"

"Sure. Maybe this time around we can just be friends."

"I'd like that." Brighton stood, crossed the room to the bed, and thrust his hand forward. "Hi. My name is Brighton Stansbury. You know nothing about me, but you look like a nice person. Want to be my friend?"

Merri laughed and instead of shaking his hand, she stuck the plate of cookies in it. "My name is Merri Wilcox. You look a little crazy, but yes, I'll be your friend. Want a cookie?"

"The roads are open!" Brighton called as he burst into the kitchen an hour later. Nana and Merri sat at the table, playing a game of Rook. "They just announced it on the news. I'm calling a tow truck right now. Merri, looks like you'll be home for Christmas after all."

"I can't wait." The idea of being with Nicole's family made her happy, yet the idea of leaving Nana left sadness, too.

Brighton disappeared into the living room and reappeared twenty minutes later. "I think that's the longest time I've ever spent on hold. I had to pay extra, but I finally found someone willing to move us to the top of their list. They'll get the car and bring it to us here." Brighton looked at Merri with questioning eyes. She knew he wondered if his monetary influence would bother her, but she also knew he only did it because he wanted to get her home in time for Christmas.

She smiled warmly so he knew she didn't mind. "How long will it take?"

"Probably a couple of hours. I'm going to keep shoveling."

Merri jumped up from the table. "I'll come with you." Although she loved Nana's company, she had to admit that the snowball fight with Brighton had been the highlight of her day. At least, before it ended in a fight of words.

"Sounds like the perfect time for me to take a nap," Nana said.

The pair bundled up yet again and stepped outside. The clouds had completely cleared and the late afternoon sun reflected off the snow. It wouldn't be long before it set. The sound of an approaching engine came toward them through the trees.

"That can't be the tow truck already, can it?" Merri asked.

Brighton shook his head. "It sounds like a snowmobile to me,"

The two watched as, sure enough, a snowmobile with a single rider emerged from the trees and stopped next to them on the front walk. The man approached. "I'm Dan Wheeler. I live up the road."

"I'm a family friend of Angela," Brighton said. "I think I met you once before."

Angela. So that's Nana's name, Merri thought.

"Stansbury, right?" Dan asked.

Brighton nodded.

"I'm the one that clears Angela's drive for her after a storm. I've got a plow on my truck. I thought I'd stop by and check on her before I got started."

"She's doing great, just taking a nap."

"Good," Dan said as he climbed back onto his snowmobile. "I'll get started then. Tell her to call me if she needs anything."

"It's nice that the neighbors watch out for Nana," Merri said as she watched Dan drive off.

"Everyone loves her," Brighton said.

"It's hard not to."

They returned to the job of shoveling the snow off

the walk. Knowing they wouldn't have to shovel the half mile drive made it easier to work. Within half an hour, they had the entire front walk and wraparound porch completely cleared. They'd chatted while they worked, careful not to bring up the subject of high school or past behavior. As Merri threw the last shovelful of snow from the section where she worked, she turned to see why Brighton had grown so quiet. He knelt in the snow, forming a huge snowball.

"You've got to be kidding me. You're not going to throw that at me, are you?" Merri asked fearfully.

"This," Brighton said without looking up, "is the beginning of the world's best snowman."

"I see. Want some help?"

"I planned on it."

The pair labored together to build a snowman, stretching to get the last ball in place as the head of the snowman. The heavy snow was perfect for building and shaping. As a result, each segment of the snowman came out perfectly round. By the time they finished, the snowman had pinecone buttons and eyes with pine needle eyebrows and mouth.

"See. We work well together," Brighton said. His words were accompanied by a raise of his eyebrows and Merri couldn't help but wonder if a question hid behind them.

She ignored the nagging in her brain. "Earlier we had a snowball fight and then you tried to whitewash me with snow. Now, we've built a snowman. Any other childish activities you want to accomplish while I'm already a frozen wet mess?"

"Hmm..." Brighton's eyes sparkled. "I've got an idea." He pushed himself up from the snow and offered a hand to Merri. She took it, but let go as soon as she had her footing.

"Follow me," he instructed.

"Where are we going?"

"You'll see. Just trust me."

"I think you said something along those lines when you invited me up here for a *quick* trip to cut Nana's hair."

Brighton sighed dramatically. "I'm never going to be forgiven for this, am I?"

"You're already forgiven. But that doesn't mean I'm going to stop making you relive the shame." She nudged him with her shoulder and then instantly regretted her action. *Why can't I stop flirting with him?*

Brighton led Merri to the wraparound front porch. They'd cleared all the snow from it so they were able to easily walk around it to the back of the house. "The snow back here is completely untouched," he said.

"So?"

"It's better that way."

"Better for what?"

"This."

Merri's mouth fell open in surprise as Brighton climbed to the top of the railing. "What are you doing?"

"Just follow my lead," Brighton instructed. "The technique will all come flooding back."

Brighton glanced at her one more time before yelling "Bombs away!" and leaping from the railing to the mounds of untouched snow below.

Merri gasped. "Are you crazy?"

"The key is to jump out as far as you can. The finished product looks more authentic that way." Brighton laid down in the snow and began moving his arms and legs back and forth, forming a perfect snow angel.

"Ah...now I get it."

"Your turn."

Merri turned to the kitchen window, wondering if Nana watched their craziness, but she couldn't see her. She probably still napped. And it did look fun... Merri climbed to the top of the railing and took a deep breath. "No laughing," she called as she leaped as far out into the snow as she could, making sure to leave plenty of room between her angel and Brighton's. She copied his arm and leg flapping until she produced a matching angel. They both jumped back to the porch and pulled themselves up, admiring their work.

"Not bad," Brighton said. "Want to go again?" He looked at Merri, but then frowned. "You're shivering."

"I think I'm wetter now than when we first arrived yesterday after walking in the storm."

"Let's go inside. The tow truck will probably be here soon anyway."

The kitchen door was locked so the pair circled back to the front door and let themselves in, stomping the loose snow on the entryway rug before removing their boots. The smell of the molasses cookies still hung thick in the air and Merri inhaled deeply. "It smells like Christmas."

They laid their wet coats and boots and gloves by the fire again and Merri found herself longing for Nana's bathrobe and the comfort of the log bed. She stuck her hands out in front of the fire to warm them, but she still shivered.

"You're freezing," Brighton said. "Sorry I kept you out there so long." He put his hands on her arms and rubbed them up and down, trying to warm her. Merri's heart caught in her throat at his touch. For a moment, they both stared at each other in complete silence. She stopped shivering.

"I thought I heard the door." Nana's voice came from behind them.

Brighton dropped his hands immediately and turned away. Merri glanced down at her shirt, convinced that everyone in the room could see her heart pounding through her chest.

"Ready for some cookies and milk?" Nana asked. "I've got it all poured.

"Have I ever told you that you're the best?" Brighton gave Nana a hug as he passed her on the way into the kitchen.

"By the way, Bright," Nana said as she followed him into the kitchen. "The tow company called while you were out. They found your car and were in the process of pulling it out. They should be here soon."

Merri frowned. The words should have made her happy, but for some reason she couldn't feel anything but disappointment.

Chapter 10

"Goodbye, Nana. Thanks for letting me into your home these last couple of days," Merri said as she hugged the elderly woman. The tow company had delivered Brighton's SUV and after a good brushing, it was clear of snow and warming in the driveway.

"It was my pleasure. I hope I get to see you again," Nana said with a glance toward Brighton.

"I'd like that," Merri said. "I'll cut your hair anytime you want."

She tossed her purse and duffel bag into the backseat and climbed into the front of the car while Brighton said his goodbyes.

"Try to keep it on the road this time," Merri teased as Brighton eased himself into the driver's seat.

"Come on, this adventure hasn't been all bad, has it?"

"I guess I'm still in one piece."

The roads going out of the canyon and back into the valley were still packed with ice and snow and Brighton drove slowly as he worked his way out of the mountains. Merri didn't mind him being overly cautious. They chatted while they drove and she felt like she learned more about the real Brighton during that drive than she did in all the years of being in school together. She knew the moment they'd entered an area with cell reception because Brighton's phone beeped over and over, announcing that he had an entire selection of missed calls and texts to choose from. Her phone's battery had long since died. The time without it had been surprisingly nice.

Merri glanced down at Brighton's glowing phone on the console between them. Sixteen missed texts and eight missed calls—all from some girl named Lizzie. Her heart jumped in her chest.

Brighton has a girlfriend. Why wouldn't he?

Her mind raced and she tried to think back to all the conversations they'd had over the last two days, hoping she hadn't said anything too embarrassing. *It never even crossed my mind that he might not be single. She's probably been worried sick about him since he couldn't call. I hope I didn't come off too flirty. And I'm so glad I didn't ask him out like Nana suggested.*

Back at Nana's, they'd agreed to be friends. Nothing more. Although she'd developed an unexplained and surprising fondness for Brighton over the last two days, Merri knew it had to end there. She'd forgiven the one person she held a grudge against and that made her life better.

So why do I feel sad?

Finally, as they neared the downtown area and *The Cut* where she'd left her car, Merri decided she had to get one last thing off her chest before leaving Brighton's presence. "Nana told me why you work for your dad," she said quietly. "I just thought you should know."

Brighton didn't say anything for a few moments. When he finally spoke, his voice was hesitant. "How much detail did she give?"

"How much detail is there?"

A small smile played on Brighton's lips. "That depends."

"She told me you started your own company, but didn't have enough money to get it off the ground. You agreed to work for your dad for ten years in exchange for the startup cash." Merri paused. "She also told me you worked your way through college and paid for your own schooling."

"Did she also tell you I failed miserably when I tried to start my company?"

"Not in those words."

"You successfully started your own salon. I hate to admit it, but I'm jealous."

"Starting a small salon is a lot different than a big company like you were doing. I hope you know that Nana's proud of you for doing it." Merri stopped to take a deep breath. "And I am, too. I mean, you could have worked for your dad right from the start, but instead you took a chance on one of your dreams."

"Yeah, well, I didn't make it very long before I came crawling back to dear old Dad."

"It's only temporary."

"Ten years is a long time."

"True. But think of it as a time to grow closer to your family. You said your siblings are a lot older than you. If you're working with them now, you must be getting to know them better."

Brighton snorted. "They still think of me as a child, even though I hold a higher degree than either of them. Their business practices aren't always ethical in my opinion, and I include my dad in that statement. Believe me, we're not a family that goes on joint vacations and eats Sunday dinner together every week."

"I'm sorry."

"Do you see why I spent so much time at Nana's as a child?"

"I assumed it was all about her amazing cooking, but yeah, I'm starting to understand now."

Brighton reached forward and pounded a fist on the dashboard. Merri jumped at the sound. "Dad insists I drive company-provided cars like this one and stay in a company-provided apartment just to make himself look more impressive. I don't feel like I've actually earned any of this stuff, you know? People meet me and they hear my last name and assume they know everything about me. I want to be my own person, not just Richard Stansbury's son. If I can just stick it out long enough, I'll have the money to break free and do what I want."

"I have faith in you. You'll accomplish your goal. And meanwhile, I'm not going to judge you for working for your dad."

Brighton smiled and looked over at her. "You don't know how much that means to me. I meant what I said before about you being the only person that saw me for me."

"This is my stop, I guess," Merri said as Brighton parked at the curb in front of her salon.

Brighton got out of the car and circled around to

the passenger side. "Want me to carry your bag for you?"

"I can get it. I'm just going to get in my car without actually going inside."

"I guess this is goodbye then."

Merri nodded. "Goodbye. Thanks for the adventure." She started to turn away, but stopped when Brighton reached out and touched her shoulder. He gave her a small hug, but she tried not to read too much into it, knowing he had a girlfriend. "I'll see you around." That time, she stepped away and didn't look back.

Opening the door to her apartment didn't bring as much satisfaction as she thought it would. Usually, entering her home after a tiring day at work was an action she thoroughly enjoyed, but that night, after Brighton dropped her off, Merri felt the loneliness more than ever.

"After two days of people to talk to, I'm going through withdrawals," she said aloud as she sprinkled fish food into the bowl on the table. "What do you think, Bomber? Am I crazy for talking to you? What about you, Betsy? If you can understand me, wave your fin." The fish didn't do anything and she could only stand hovering over their bowl for a few moments before returning the fish food to the cabinet.

Merri walked into the living room area and plugged in the lights to her tiny Christmas tree. The tree stood barely three feet, but on top of an end table it reached two more. The red, sparkling lights reminded her of the lights surrounding Nana's home and she smiled at the memory, hoping she would get the opportunity to see the elderly woman again.

A half hour later, Merri had taken a much needed shower and changed into fuzzy pajama bottoms and an oversized sweatshirt. It wasn't her most flattering look, but it was by far the most comfortable outfit she had.

She checked her newly charged phone. She didn't have nearly as many missed calls as Brighton had on his. In fact, there were only four. Two from Nicole, one from her parents, and one from Paige.

"Hey, Nicole," Merri said when her sister answered her phone.

"You finally have your phone. Are you home?"

"I just got home a little while ago."

"Are you coming over tonight?"

"Aren't the kids already in bed?"

"Not yet. We let them stay up late since it's Christmas Eve."

"Would you be offended if I didn't come over until Christmas morning. I promise to be there in time for them to open their presents. I'm really tired."

"I don't mind. I'm sure hanging out with Brighton was exhausting."

"What's that supposed to mean?"

"You always stress out when you're around him."

"I do not."

Nicole didn't say anything.

"Fine. I do." Merri smiled to herself. "We worked some things out. I think we're done fighting with each other."

"If you're not fighting, does that mean you're...together?"

"No. Absolutely not." Merri shook her head emphatically even though Nicole couldn't see her through the phone. "We just agreed to be friends. Brighton has a girlfriend anyway. And judging by the number of times she tried to call him while we were out of cell range, it's pretty serious."

"*How very disappointing. I wanted you to finally hook up with him so you'd have access to all that money. Just think of the sister trips we could go on if you were rich.*"

"You're shallow."

"*I know. Anyway, the kids are waiting for me to read them a Christmas story before bed. I'll see you in the morning. 'Night.*"

"Goodnight."

Merri hung up her phone and tossed it on the couch. She turned on the TV and flipped through the channels, but it seemed that every station played Christmas movies. Normally, she wouldn't mind them—in fact, she'd pop some popcorn and enjoy them—but that year she couldn't bring herself to watch the feel good movies where families always end up together for the holidays when she felt so alone. "I should have given in and gone to St. George to be with Mom and Dad," she muttered to herself.

As she sat, her mind wandered to the events of the last few days. As much as she didn't want to admit it to herself, spending time with Brighton—and Nana— had been the highlight of her week, maybe even her month. But there was more she didn't want to admit—a feeling she tried to suppress. Finally, with *It's A Wonderful Life* playing in the background, she whispered, "I'm falling for Brighton Stansbury."

As if on cue, a knock sounded on Merri's

apartment door, pulling her from her thoughts. She shook herself, shocked about what she'd just admitted to herself, and crossed the room to the door. She looked through the peephole before removing the chain and unlocking the deadbolt. A man stood in the hallway with his back to her. He wore a stocking hat, but she recognized the figure. "I swear Shawn said he wouldn't come back until after the holidays. The poor guy must be as bored as I am," she muttered to herself as she opened the door for her shy neighbor.

The figure turned around. "Merri."

She gasped. "Brighton! I thought you were...someone else." Suddenly self-conscious, she tucked her damp hair behind her ears and looked down at her fuzzy pajama pants. Yep. She'd lost all dignity. "What are you doing here? Did I leave something in your car?" She looked at his hands to see what he carried. They were both stuffed in his pockets.

"I probably shouldn't have come, but I couldn't stop thinking about you after I left. I had to come back to talk to you before I chickened out." Brighton had obviously showered and changed, too. His face, that only an hour before bore the stubble of two days without a razor, was soft and smooth.

Merri resisted the urge to touch his face. "What about Lizzie? Isn't she worried about you?"

Brighton narrowed his eyes. "Why would Lizzie be worried about me?"

"Because you've been gone for two days. If my boyfriend disappeared during the holidays and didn't return my calls or texts I'd be losing my mind."

"I'm so confused."

"Your phone. I saw all the missed calls from her."

A slow smile spread across Brighton's face. "Lizzie's not my girlfriend."

"Come on, no girl calls a guy that much in two day's time unless it's serious. You might not think she's your girlfriend, but I'd be willing to bet she thinks otherwise."

"I'll take that bet." Brighton stuck his hand toward Merri.

She hesitated, suddenly unsure.

Brighton laughed. "Lizzie is my sister. All her calls and texts were work related. Oh, except for the one that said...hold on a sec." Brighton pulled his phone from his pants pocket and turned it on. Merri watched silently as he scanned for something. "Here it is. 'Are you going somewhere on Christmas day? 'If you don't have plans and really need a place to go, I guess you can come over for dinner.'"

"Ouch."

Brighton shrugged. "Now you know why I spend all my time with Nana. She might not be blood-related, but she's the closest thing to family I've got."

"So...what did you come here to tell me?"

Brighton looked over her shoulder. "Do you mind if I come in?"

The pair still stood in the doorway. "Of course. Sorry. I'm not used to people coming to my door." *Except Shawn, and he won't cross the threshold.* "If I'd known you were coming back, I would have dressed in normal clothes after I showered, and maybe put some makeup on."

"I kind of like this look." Brighton reached up and tucked a loose strand of damp hair behind her ear, but then quickly dropped his hand. "You have fish?" he said, crossing the room to the fish bowl.

"I wanted a pet, but I can't have dogs here. And I didn't want to be a cat lady. Sadly, Bomber and Betsy—the fish—aren't as entertaining as I'd hoped."

Brighton grinned. "I just got a puppy a couple of weeks ago. You can play with him anytime you want."

"I'll keep that in mind the next time I'm bored."

The pair sat down in kitchen chairs. Merri still couldn't figure out why Brighton had returned so she sat silently until he finally spoke.

"There's something I wanted to say earlier today, but I didn't. I should have, but... Anyway, we've known each other for a really long time and I feel like I really know you and..." Brighton stared at his hands while he spoke.

His nervousness put Merri on edge. "And?"

"And I hoped that you'd consider dating me. I really like you Merri Wilcox. I think I always have."

Merri's heart pounded in her chest. She didn't know what to say. His revelation was the last think she expected. Brighton finally looked up at her. All his feelings showed on his face. They were sincere.

"I'd like that—a lot."

Brighton let out a rush of air. "It's like a huge burden was just lifted from my shoulders."

Merri laughed. "I agree. I think we've both been in denial. And that's really hard to admit."

Brighton reached forward and entwined his fingers with hers. It felt right to Merri. "Now what do we do?" he asked.

"You mean you didn't come with a plan in mind?"

"I didn't want to plan too far ahead in case you rejected me and kicked me to the curb."

Merri nodded toward the TV still playing in the living room. "*It's A Wonderful Life* is on. Want to eat popcorn and watch it?"

"Sounds perfect." He paused. "Wait, weren't you going to your sister's house tonight?"

"No. I told her I'd come over tomorrow. You're welcome to come with me. My niece and nephews are a riot."

"I'd like that—if you're sure your sister won't mind."

"Trust me. She'd be elated."

Merri stood and walked toward the couch, pulling Brighton with her, but he held back. "Hold on a second. I left something in the hall."

Merri raised her eyebrows but didn't say anything as Brighton stepped back outside her door. He came back in with one hand tucked behind his back. "There's not many stores open at this time of night on Christmas Eve, and I didn't have a clue where to start looking, so I hoped this would work." He pulled his hand from behind his back and revealed a small pine bough tied with a red ribbon. He held the bough above his head. "You mentioned how much you like the smell of pine. I thought maybe this could be a substitute for mistletoe."

Merri's mouth dropped open and she laughed. "You knew all along that I wouldn't reject you, didn't you?"

Brighton shrugged. "I hoped, but..."

He couldn't finish his sentence because Merri stepped forward then, standing on tiptoes to meet his lips. Sweet and gentle, the kiss would be burned into her memory for a long time. It just felt right. And sitting on the couch that night, with Brighton's arm wrapped around her as they watched *It's A Wonderful Life*, she knew she'd truly found *her* wonderful life.

ABOUT THE AUTHOR

Author Tifani Clark grew up on a farm in southeastern Idaho (yes, that's where they grow all the potatoes) as the middle of five children. She had a lot of space to imagine and daydream and often pictured hers elf as a character in one of the many books she read. She was habitually found pretending to be Scarlet O'Hara. She is married to the love of her life and is the mother to four fabulous children. When not writing, she enjoys playing the violin and piano and traveling to new places. She especially enjoys visits to national parks and places of historical significance.